A lifelong history buff, **Georgie Lee** hasn't given up hope that she will one day inherit a title and a manor house. Until then she fulfils her dreams of lords, ladies and a Season in London through her stories. When not writing she can be found reading non-fiction history or watching any film with a costume and an accent. Please visit georgie-lee.com to learn more about Georgie and her books.

Also by Georgie Lee

The Cinderella Governess
Captain Rose's Redemption

The Business of Marriage miniseries

A Debt Paid in Marriage
A Too Convenient Marriage
The Secret Marriage Pact

Scandal and Disgrace miniseries

Rescued from Ruin
Miss Marianne's Disgrace
Courting Danger with Mr Dyer

Discover more at millsandboon.co.uk.

HIS MISTLETOE MARCHIONESS

Georgie Lee

MILLS & BOON

This is a work of fiction. Names, characters, places, locations
and incidents are purely fictional and bear no relationship to
any real life individuals, living or dead, or to any actual places,
business establishments, locations, events or incidents.
Any resemblance is entirely coincidental.

First Published in Great Britain 2018
by Mills & Boon, an imprint of HarperCollins*Publishers*
1 London Bridge Street, London, SE1 9GF

ISBN: 978-0-263-93325-3

This ... er

F...

To my wonderful readers,
may you have a happy and hope-filled Christmas season.

Chapter One

Kent, England—December 20th, 1806

'I still can't believe you talked me into coming back to Stonedown Manor for Christmas,' Lady Clara Kingston complained to Lady Anne Exton, her sister-in-law, for the second time during their journey. The first had been when they'd set out two hours ago from their estate, Winsome Manor. Conversation with Anne had eased Clara's initial misgivings and for a while the carriage ride through the snow-covered countryside had been soothing. But as the rolling hills of Surrey had changed to the flatter lands on the edges of the Weald in Kent and the familiar landscape surrounding Stonedown Manor, Clara's apprehension had returned. With Stonedown looming on a nearby rise, the creamy stone front of it fading into the stark and leafless trees and frost-covered hills behind it, Clara's unease increased.

'You're too young to cloister yourself at Winsome,' Anne said. 'And what better way to return to society than surrounded by people you know who will be glad to see you? It's been ages since you've attended one of Lord and Lady Tillman's annual Christmas house parties.'

'For good reason.' It'd been six years since the last time Clara had travelled this road. Back then she'd been heading home with the disappointment and embarrassment that had marred the remaining days of that Christmas visit accompanying her. It had been one of the worst Christmases that she'd ever endured and one of the best and most memorable.

'That was a long time ago, Clara, and far behind you. Think of the better times,' Anne encouraged.

'I'm trying.' Clara traced the outline of her wedding ring beneath her glove. She'd been unable to take it off despite the two years that had come and gone since Alfred's passing. With him beside her, she could have returned to Stonedown without the regrets and doubts weighing her down, laughing at the less-than-pleasant memories of her last visit instead of allowing them to torture her as much as his loss. The surety of his love and protection was no longer there to help her and never would be again. Whatever waited for her at Stonedown, she must face it alone, as she had the humiliation that had marked that Christmas morning six years ago before Alfred's caring had driven it away.

Clara nearly rapped on the roof of the coach to tell the driver to turn around and take her back to Winsome, but instead she clasped her hands tight together in her lap, her wedding ring pushing into the crook of her fingers. She couldn't run away from this like a scared spinster or that was exactly what she would become. She was tired of being the widowed aunt, of living through Anne's and Adam's lives while hers remained mired by a loss of love and purpose. This more than all of Anne's urgings had brought her to Stonedown. After two years secluded in the country, even she could see how the isolation and loneliness weren't good for her.

Anne leaned across the carriage and

clasped Clara's hands, giving them a reassuring squeeze. 'Don't worry, Clara. Everything will be all right. You'll enjoy yourself and who knows what might happen. You met Alfred here. There might be someone equally special waiting for you this time.'

The light of hope in Anne's pale green eyes surprised Clara as much as the sensation rising in her heart. Hoping for such a thing felt like a betrayal of Alfred's memory, but she needed to believe that there was something more waiting for her than the endless lonely days at Winsome Manor, many of which she spent lamenting what hadn't been. Alfred wouldn't want her to stop living, but the chance of lightning striking twice at Stonedown was remote, as was the possibility that she and others would not recall that her biggest embarrassment had also happened here. 'Assuming people can see me as I am and not always think of me the way I was and what happened before.'

'Few people will be so bored during their time here as to dwell on that unfortunate incident. There's no reason for anyone to remember or to bring it up.'

'I pray you're right.' Clara didn't wish for

people to view her as the simple girl who'd allowed herself to be duped by a fortune hunter, but as the poised Marchioness of Kingston that she'd become in the years since. It was the other reason she'd decided to come here, to prove to herself and everyone how much she'd changed. As for love finding her twice at Stonedown, she wasn't that hopeful. 'I doubt there will be anyone waiting at the house party for me. Most of the guests our age are married and the rest are old enough to be our parents. But you're right, this is a good chance for me to venture out again and remember what it's like.'

'Don't be too safe,' Anne suggested with a mischievous smile as she sat back against the squabs. 'An innocent risk every now and then is good for a woman.'

The plotting look in Anne's eyes made Clara wonder if Anne knew something about Lady Tillman's guest list that she didn't. There wasn't time to ask as the carriage made the turn on to the main drive leading to the massive front staircase.

A number of other carriages stood before the entrance, disgorging their passengers who strode up the numerous steps to the house.

Spying the carriages and all the familiar faces, the excitement and anticipation that used to seize Clara when she and Adam were children and their parents would bring them here for the week before Christmas swept her again. Yes, she would enjoy herself in a way she hadn't done in years and perhaps for a little while forget the lingering sadness that had been draping her for far too long.

A footman opened the carriage door and a gust of cool air with a hint of snow rushed in. Clara stepped out and peered up at the tall façade and the wide columns stretching up to support the triangle-shaped entrance giving Stonedown Manor the appearance of a Greek temple. It had seemed so much taller when she'd been a child holding on tight to her mother's hand while they'd climbed these same steps. Coming to Stonedown had been as much a family tradition as Christmas pudding or carols. After their parents' passing eight years ago, Clara and Adam had continued to come to Stonedown, to keep the tradition and their memory alive until that awful Christmas six years ago.

With a sigh, she started her ascent, but Anne took her by the arm, giggling like a new maid. 'Do you remember how old Lady Pariston used to pinch the footmen on the cheeks?'

Clara tossed back her head and laughed, having quite forgotten. 'I do. Didn't she catch one on the bottom once?'

'She said her shoulder hurt too much for her to reach the higher cheek. She will be here.'

'Then no footman is safe.'

They almost doubled over in laughter when they reached the top, the old memory and the chance to see the charming Dowager again giving new life to the prospect of being here. It didn't have to be all pain and regret, and Anne was right, Clara must think about the happy memories instead of dwelling on the unfortunate ones.

She and Anne stepped into the main entrance hall and craned their necks to take in the tall-ceilinged room with wide-eyed wonder. Despite the marble floors, the stone and iron of the curving front stairs and the high plastered ceilings and stark white moulding, there was a cosiness to Stonedown, an air of family and comfortable living one often didn't find in estates this grand. This was the seat of the Earls of Tillman, but also their true home and, where it once rang with the noise of their five children, it now echoed with the sound of their grandchildren and the children of the guests and all the people gathered to celebrate Christmas. Fresh boughs of holly adorned every table and garlands of evergreens draped the long banister of the wide staircase leading up to the first floor. The crisp and spicy scent of cinnamon and nutmeg mingled with the earthy aroma of pine while the tinkling notes of someone playing Christmas carols on the piano in the music room drifted through the air. Clara took it all in, allowing the many happy memories of Christmases with her family here to fill her and make her doubts about coming fade. This delight was exactly what her tired soul needed.

'There's Lady Tillman. She will be so happy to see you.' Anne guided her to where their stately hostess stood beneath a magnificent painting of the Italian countryside.

Lady Tillman, with her grey hair done up and decorated with a sprig of holly, and her thick figure regal in a dark green velvet frock with long sleeves and fur cuffs, reminded

Clara of her mother and the way she used to appear whenever she'd greeted house party guest at Winsome Manor. The Countess smiled while she watched a group of children race past her. One of the little boys bumped into a half-pillar and made the vase on top of it rattle, causing the footman near it to leap at the ceramic to make sure it didn't fall. Lady Tillman uttered not one word of reprimand, the near loss of a vase a worthy price to pay to have this much joy echoing off the overhead frescos.

Clara watched the children dart between the guests, the ribbons of the little girls' dresses fluttering while the shoes of their brothers and cousins and friends slapped against the stone. Clara smiled at the sight, but it slowly faded as the familiar sadness she'd endured too many times in the past six years dropped over her like a blanket. At one time she'd dreamed of returning here for Christmas with a son or daughter who could play with her niece and nephew and enjoy the festive season the same way she had as a child but it hadn't been. As with his first wife, she and Alfred had had no children. With Alfred gone, her dreams of having a family of her own were in danger of never coming true and it left a hole in her heart that made her want to weep.

'Lady Kingston, Lady Exton, how magnificent to see you both.' Lady Tillman strode up to Anne and Clara. Clara struggled to push aside her melancholy and greet their hostess. This wasn't the time to cry and lament. She'd done enough of that at Winsome and there would be plenty of opportunities when she was alone in her room at night, but no matter how much she smiled, she couldn't shake off the sadness completely. Alfred wasn't even here to comfort her. 'Lady Kingston, you don't know how thrilled I was when Lady Exton told me you were coming. You've been away from my parties for far too long.'

She wagged a reprimanding finger at Clara before clasping Clara's hands, her gracious and heartfelt greeting soothing Clara's sadness. 'You're right, Lady Tillman, and it's a mistake I intend to rectify.'

'You already have.' Lady Tillman patted her hand, then let go. 'You both must go on through to the dining room and have your tea before the children eat all the tarts. The little cherubs, how I adore having them here.'

'Are my children somewhere in this crush?' Anne glanced about to see if she could spy the tow-haired heads of James and Lillie.

'Oh, yes, they went running through here some time ago and your husband is in the billiards room with Lord Tillman and many of the other men.'

There hadn't been enough room in the carriage for them all so Adam and the children had gone on ahead while Anne had ridden with Clara. Clara felt sure she'd done it to offer her support and she was thankful for the company, especially as they waded through the guests on their way to the dining room. Clara gave and accepted greetings from many old acquaintances, all the while enduring their consolations. It made her feel loved and wanted, but even these kind words reminded her of the loss of Alfred and how grief had made her stay away. It was a bittersweet arrival.

'Lady Kingston, is that you?' Lady Pariston stopped them. Wisps of her grey hair stuck out from beneath her white lace mobcap and she stooped a bit where she gripped a walking stick in her frail hands. Clara had never remembered her as robust or young, but she seemed even older today, but no less cheerful than she'd been before. Nothing ever appeared to dampen the Dowager Countess's delight in everything. Lady Pariston leaned forward on her stick with a little too much amusement and no small amount of mirth. 'What trouble do you intend to get up to this time, Lady Kingston? Plan to get jilted by another marquess while you're here? I don't think there are any in attendance, and if there happens to be more than one then you must share. It was awful of you to keep both of them to yourself last time, even if you did land the better of the two.'

Clara stiffened, struggling to maintain her smile. 'I'll be sure to share this time if there's more than one marquess.'

'Good. I know you won't believe it to look at me, but I used to have to fend off marquesses, and even a duke, with a stick.' While Lady Pariston waxed on about her past, Clara glanced around to see if any footmen stood in danger of her fingers, but none was so close. 'If I hadn't loved Charles so much I never would have consented to becoming a mere countess, but he more than made up for the step down by the size of his manor.'

She nudged Clara with her elbow and Clara laughed.

'A sizeable manor does make a great deal of difference, doesn't it?' Clara could enjoy Lady Pariston's jokes because they were not cruelly meant. She spoke plainly and frankly and expected everyone around her to do the same.

'I'll say. Now go on through to your tea and pick out the man you want to catch this time.'

Lady Pariston strolled off, her gait, despite the walking stick, as spry as her laugh.

Clara crossed her arms and trilled her fingers on them as she turned to Anne. 'So much for no one remembering that unfortunate incident from the last time I was here.'

'Well, if anyone was going to bring up what happened, you know it would be Lady Pariston.'

'I doubt she'll be the only one.' Clara nodded to where Lady Fulton in her lace-cuffed dress that did little to contain her large chest and slender Lord Westbook with his sharp nose and slicked-back dark hair stood whispering together, each of them throwing Clara sidelong glances and then casually strolling away when it was clear that they'd been seen. Clara was certain they were not discussing the size of her diamond earrings. 'What was it that Lady Fulton called me? A plain country mouse?'

'And you are no longer that any more. Chin up, my dear Marchioness. There are tarts to eat.'

They strolled to the dining room, their progress slowed by more greetings, and Clara tried to shake her irritation at Lady Fulton and Lord Westbook. Their catty remarks had made a bad situation much worse six years ago and, unlike Lady Pariston's silly and innocent reminder of Clara's past, she knew anything they said was designed to inflict the most damage. The two of them were notorious gossips and Clara's story must have greatly amused them, and who knew how many other country families six years ago.

As if to add insult to injury, it was then that she and Anne passed the small hallway leading to the ballroom. A sprig of mistletoe hung from the chandelier in the centre of the hallway, just as it did every year. Clara paused, noticing the white berries adorning the branch, and the memory of that Christmas Eve six years rushed back to her…

'We should probably return to the ballroom,' Hugh had suggested, rocking back on his heels before planting himself firmly in front of her.

'Yes, we wouldn't want people to notice our absence and talk.'

She didn't care if they did. She yearned to stay there in the hallway beneath the mistletoe alone with him. He must desire it, too, for neither of them made a move to return to the dancing and she enjoyed this rush of boldness, the first one she'd ever experienced in a man's presence.

He stepped forward and clasped her hands in his.

She straightened, struggling to stand still against the excitement coursing through her at the press of his fingers against hers.

His pulse flickered beneath her grasp and a shiver of excitement made her tremble. She wished to feel not just his fingertips against her skin but the entirety of him and everything promised by the longing in his eyes.

He wanted her as much as she wanted him,

not in the sordid way spoken of in gossip, but in a deep and binding union of their lives…

Until the next morning, Clara thought wryly, the memory of crushing the berry he'd plucked for her from the mistletoe beneath her boot heel in the drive the next morning equally potent. Hugh might not have asked for her hand in so many words, but it had been there in every look he'd cast her that night and across the table and sitting rooms of the days before. The ones everyone in the house had seen, too. How people like Lady Fulton had sneered at her when Hugh had left to marry another. Despite his kiss and everything they'd shared that week, she'd been nothing more to him than a way to pass the time until someone more lucrative had come along and she'd been too much of a simple country girl to see it.

Clara swept off to follow Anne into the dining room. *I'm not that naïve girl any more.*

And she would make sure that people like Lady Fulton recognised it.

'Oh, Clara, Lady Tillman has set out her mincemeat tarts.' Anne eyed Lady Worth's small china plate as she passed them. 'I must have one before they're all gone for it isn't the start of the Christmas season until I've eaten one.'

'Don't you wish to greet your husband?' Clara was somewhat curious to venture into the billiards room and see what men were in attendance, almost ashamed to admit she did hold out some hope for this party. After all, it was the season of miracles and she could do with one.

'Adam can wait. The tarts will not.' Anne took a tart from the magnificent selection of treats arranged on the long table and enjoyed a large bite, sighing at the sweet taste and the aromatic holiday spices.

'You're right.' Clara took a bite of her selection, savouring the cinnamon-laced confection. 'It isn't Christmas until I've had one of these.'

Anne dabbed the sides of her mouth with a small napkin, then set it on the tray of a passing footman. 'No, it isn't. Oh, there's Adam. I must tell him that I brought his cufflinks and will have my maid send them to his valet. I'll be right back.'

She rushed off to take care of this domestic matter, leaving Clara to enjoy more tarts. While she finished her last treat, her stays already growing tight from the bounty of delights, she noticed the open door to Lord Tillman's library across the hall from the dining room. Through the white-corniced frame, she could see the warm fire burning in the grate, its light glistening off the many gold-tooled titles of the books lining the walls. If there was one other Christmas tradition she could not do without, it was perusing Lord Tillman's illuminated manuscript outlining the Nativity, the one he set out every year for his guests to enjoy. The last time she'd admired the Nativity had been six years ago when Hugh had glanced at her from across the wide pages, his fingers brushing hers when he'd turned the aged parchment. It had been the place where Hugh had first become more to her than her elder brother's long-time friend and sometime houseguest at Winsome Manor and everything between them had changed.

No, I will not think about that, but of better times.

She left the bright dining room and crossed the hall to the library. It was just as she remembered it, with the shelves filled with antique manuscripts and more recent novels. The heaviness of the wood bookshelves and mouldings and the dark leather of the furniture made the room much darker than any of the others in the house, but with a large fire burning in the grate and the medieval illuminated manuscript perched on the tall bookstand by the window, it was one of the cosiest places in Stonedown. Lord Tillman was generous with his collection, making everything in it available to his guests. She'd spent many hours in this room with her father during the Christmases when he'd been alive, with him helping her to puzzle through the Latin text of the manuscript or to select a novel to read while she was here. She would take the book up to her room and every night before falling asleep she'd devour a few pages, relaxing after the excitement of the festive days. The next day at breakfast, she and her father would discuss the story, for he always urged her to choose ones he'd already read and he would make her guess how it might end. She used to beg him to tell her, but he never would spoil the story no matter how well he knew it or whether or not it was one of his favourites.

Taking a deep breath of the smoke-tinged air flavoured with the faint must of old paper, she closed her eyes and almost forgot for a moment that her father and mother were gone, and that she'd spent too many of the last eight years missing people the most at this time of year.

She opened her eyes and crossed the room to the illuminated manuscript. The sunlight coming in from outside, despite being muted by passing clouds, still sparkled in the glittering gold of the chorus of singing angels' halos and in the fine calligraphy of the first letter of the page. The book was in Latin and she peered at it, trying to make out what words she could remember from her lessons with Adam and their father so long ago. Unlike her brother, she'd never mastered the old language, but a few words and phrases were familiar and she worked them out in a whisper, her effort making the noise and chatter in the hallway and rooms outside fade away until one voice rang out above them, stopping her cold in her reading.

'Lady Kingston, it's a pleasure to see you again.'

Clara's finger froze over the red calligraphy, her pulse pounding in her ears. She took a deep breath and turned slowly around to find Hugh Almstead, Fifth Marquess of Delamare, standing at the bookshelf in the corner holding an open book. He didn't flinch at the sight of her, but his confidence was betrayed by the subtle shifting of his weight on his feet. In her eagerness to view the manuscript and to remember everything she used to love about being in this room with her father, she'd walked right past him, unaware this entire time that he'd been watching her from the shadows.

He closed the book and stood up a touch straighter. He'd gained some height and his chest had grown wider along with his shoulders since the last time she'd seen him. His dark blue coat highlighted the darker strands in his sandy brown hair and made the copper flecks in his light brown eyes stand out. He appeared more like a man than the boy who'd courted her six years ago before abandoning her for a richer woman.

She worked hard to swallow down the old anger while she straightened the line of brass buttons on the front of the spencer covering the top of her London-made mauve dress. The entire time she prayed that the shock and agitation of seeing him again didn't show on her face. No one had thought to tell her that *he* would be here. With so many other memories and feelings already leaving her raw, she didn't need his presence conjuring up more for her to struggle with. 'Lord Delamare, what a surprise to see you.'

If he was shocked by her presence, he hid it well, his piercing brown eyes taking her in with an earnestness she couldn't read. 'I find myself in need of some Christmas joy. I always remembered finding it here at Stonedown, especially in the people.'

He traced the leather corner of the book with a weariness she knew well. She'd lost interest in so many things after Alfred's death and now faced the challenge of rediscovering life instead of wallowing in sorrow. Then, when she was on the verge of reclaiming the simple pleasures of a house party at Christmas, here was Lord Delamare to remind her of more unpleasant times and the awkward young woman she'd once been who'd fallen for his deceptive charms.

She ceased her fiddling with the buttons and dropped her hands to her sides, striking as confident and regal a pose as she could muster. 'One would think London would hold more joy for a lord of your reputation than the woodlands of Kent.'

She tried to sound light, but the remark came off as sharp as the pop of sap on the logs in the fire. Given the tales she'd heard of him and his preference for London actresses in the last three years since his wife's death, he'd appeared more bent on emulating his grandfather's vices than his level-headed father's virtues.

'Not any more.' He slapped the book against his palm, chafing at the remark before regaining his former composure. 'My condolences on the passing of Lord Kingston. I met him a number of times in the House of Lords. He was one of the few men there who kept his word. He gained an admirable reputation because of it.'

'Yes, he was a very trustworthy and loyal man.' She fixed him with a pointed look. 'If only all lords possessed such integrity.'

He shoved the book back into its place on the shelf. 'Sometimes, life has a way of beating the integrity out of a person.'

'It didn't beat it out of Alfred.'

'Then he was a fortunate man, for many reasons.'

She wondered if he included her in those reasons, but she doubted it. He'd made his decision and not looked back—neither should she. She reined in her irritation, determined to be cordial and polite. It would be a long week if she didn't master that skill and her tongue in Hugh's presence. 'I'm very sorry about Lady Delamare, to be stolen away so young is a tragedy.'

He laced his fingers in front of him, running his thumb over the empty place where his wedding ring must have once been, the loss in his expression striking a chord deep inside Clara. 'Thank you.'

A log in the fireplace collapsed, sending up a sea of sparks. The scent of burning oak permeated the heavy air between them.

'My brother is here,' she offered, trying to lighten the mood with the kind of small talk she preferred to engage in with Lord Worth or any of the other guests. Except she'd never imagined she'd be chatting with Hugh of all people.

'I know.' Hugh faced her with the same stern countenance he'd worn when she'd first turned to see him. 'He wrote to me and told me that he and you would be here.'

This made her stiffen with surprise more than his having interrupted her private moment.

'Did he now?' She needed to end this conversation and have a very much needed other one with Adam and Anne as to why she hadn't merited the same warning.

'It was his letter that gave me a reason to come.' The tender yearning in his eyes struck her as hard as a well-packed snowball, but it didn't stun her enough to make her take leave of her senses.

He hadn't really loved her years ago. That he held a candle for anything more than perhaps her inheritance, which was now even more substantial than it had been before, was preposterous. Perhaps, having run through all the actresses in London, he was here for other, more lucrative amusements. The anger his grief had pushed aside slipped slowly back to her and she narrowed her eyes at him. 'In search of another heiress to help fill the family coffers? Or did you think a widow would serve you better?'

That wiped the tenderness off his face. She'd insulted him and she was glad, for the mistakes of six years ago along with Lord

Westbook's and Lady Fulton's snide whispers were not experiences she wished to repeat. 'My motives for being here are not as base as you believe.'

'I'm sure they're not as noble as you've convinced others to believe either.' She marched up to him, fingers closed into fists at her sides. The humiliation of standing before him in this very room years ago while he'd told her he'd decided to marry another instead of asking for her hand was made sharper by the rich scent of his bergamot shaving soap and his stance. He didn't so much as step back or flinch, but stood there, taking her disdain with irksome stoicism. She didn't expect him to crumble in shame, but at least he could have the temerity to blush or look away in guilt. 'Whatever your true reasons for coming here, be perfectly clear, they will not include me. Good day, Lord Delamare.'

Clara stepped around him and out of the room, pausing in the hallway to drag in a deep breath and settle the nervous tremors coursing through her. It wasn't like her to lob insults at people, but she hadn't been able to help herself. Nor was it like her to reveal to anyone so bluntly the depths of the injury they'd inflicted, but Hugh must see that she was no weak widow all too ready to run into his arms and surrender her fortune and her person to his control. The sooner he recognised the futility of coming here, the sooner he might leave and she could enjoy her week in peace. Until then, there was the matter of Lady Tillman's guests list to discuss with Anne.

Clara marched into the dining room and up to Anne. She laid a stern hand on Anne's arm, stopping her from taking another bite of her holiday delicacy. 'Lord Delamare is here.'

Anne peered at Clara from across the pastry before slowly lowering it to her plate. 'Is he now?'

Her surprise wasn't convincing.

'You knew he'd be here, didn't you?' Clara pulled her out of the dining room and down the hall to a secluded alcove adorned with a large vase filled with fragrant hothouse flowers.

Ann hesitated, giving Clara her answer before she even managed to stammer out a few weak lies. 'Well, no, not exactly. Adam told me Lady Tillman had said she'd invited him, but she gave him no indication that he'd accepted.'

Clara glanced down the hall to make sure no one, including Hugh or anyone else, was listening. 'You're lying. I can always tell because your cheeks go red.'

With Anne's fair complexion and blonde hair it was difficult for her to hide even the slightest of blushes.

'Yes, we knew,' Anne mumbled, suddenly very interested in the button on her spencer. 'Lady Tillman wrote to us about it a week ago, wanting to make sure there would be nothing awkward between the two of you. I assured her there wouldn't be.'

'Without consulting me first?'

'I was afraid if I told you, you wouldn't come and I wanted you to. I see the way you are at Winsome, and how lonely and sad you appear sometimes, especially while watching the children or when you think no one is looking, and it breaks my heart. I want you to be as happy as Adam and I are and to have children of your own and all the things you lost when Alfred died. You won't find them sitting in your room at home, but here with people.'

Clara swallowed hard. Only Anne could stop Clara from being angry at her when she should be steaming. She thought she'd been better about hiding her grief, but she hadn't if Anne and Adam had gone to such lengths to make sure she came to this house party. Anne was right. Clara had travelled to Stonedown to take her first steps towards finding a new life. She'd already seen a number of new faces among the usual guests. Perhaps one of them would be someone like Alfred with caring eyes and a trustworthy heart, the kind of man who'd readily comfort a grieving and rejected young woman one Christmas morning instead of laughing at her. That man was not Hugh.

'I realise Lord Delamare being here might be a little awkward,' Anne continued, 'but what happened between the two of you was a long time ago and since then he was happily married and so were you. There's no reason why you can't be polite and cordial to one another and no reason why his being here should spoil your week.'

Except Clara had already been less than cordial to him because he'd reminded her of the worst embarrassment she'd ever endured. This wasn't at all how she'd imagined this house party beginning. 'Even if we can be cordial to one another, more people than Lady Pariston are bound to remember what happened and bring it up, especially Lord Westbook and Lady Fulton and you know how cutting they can be. I told you what they said about me the last time we were here once the entire household heard of what happened.'

'And a great deal has changed since then.' Anne laid her hands on Clara's shoulders. 'There's no reason why they and everyone won't see anything but the confident woman before me.'

Clara wasn't so generous in her perception of what people would see when they looked at her. She hoped it was a mature marchioness, but she feared, especially with Lord Delamare present to remind them, that they'd see nothing but the awkward young girl she'd once been. No, she was no longer an easily tricked country heiress, but a woman of experience and sophistication who would not have the wool pulled over her eyes by a scheming man and she would prove it to everyone, including Hugh. 'Yes, you're right. Just because he's here doesn't mean I have to speak with him or give him more than a curtsy and any required manners. In fact, if I can avoid speaking to him entirely, I will.'

'Except that because of precedence, you'll be sitting next to him at every dinner,' Anne reminded, dropping her voice so as not to be heard by the gentlemen and ladies passing them as they went from the dining room to the billiards room.

Clara let out a frustrated sigh. If the footman hadn't already dragged her travelling trunk up the stairs to her room, and if Mary, her lady's maid, wasn't already busy arranging dresses in the wardrobe, Clara would order her clothes packed up and the trunk put back on the carriage so she could return home. Except there was nothing for her at home except more nights alone, more days spent in reading and solitude or watching James and Lillie play and regretting that she had no child to play with them. She could leave and allow the melancholy to claim her or stay and remain on this path to being out in the world and open to the possibility of love and a better life. That, and proving that she'd changed, was why she was here and she wouldn't allow Hugh to steal this from her the way he'd tried to steal her faith in herself six years ago. She intended to enjoy the season and she would. What Hugh did was immaterial to any of that.

Hugh examined the pages of the illuminated manuscript, trying to concentrate on the beautifully drawn and painted figures, but all he could see was Clara. The moment she'd entered the room, the only thing he'd been able to think about was the Christmas Eve ball when he'd held her in his arms. Her petite body had been languid against his when she'd curved into him with sighs as tender as her fingertips against his neck. Beneath the silk of her gown he'd been able to feel the press of her hips against his and when he'd caressed the line of her back, the sweep of his fingertips over the bare skin above the line of her bodice had made her shiver.

He'd sat across the table from her at Adam's family home over the years, paying her no more heed than he would the younger sibling of any of his friends. It wasn't until she'd entered Lady Tillman's sitting room at the beginning of that fateful Christmas house party, her dark blonde hair done up in ringlets and secured with red ribbons, the plain cut of her dress unable to hide her curving hips or the fullness of her breasts, that he'd viewed her as a woman. Even when dressed in the simplest of fashions, she'd taken his breath way and he'd struggled not to stare at the womanly changes that had come over her while she'd spoken about the falling wheat prices and how they plagued the major landowners. Her girlish interests had changed as much as her figure. In those few moments she'd transformed from the gangling young sister of his closest friend into a lady he couldn't take his eyes off, one worthy to become mistress of Everburgh Manor.

There hadn't been any trace of that smitten woman in the one who'd turned to face him today, her full lips opening with surprise before she'd pressed them tight together in disgust. Marriage and loss had changed her as much as it had changed him. The simple young woman he'd fallen for had matured, her plain country styles exchanged for the elegance of London fashion, her once-adoring looks now cutting, but he deserved her anger. It was the grief he'd seen when she'd pored over the vellum that she didn't deserve.

He turned the manuscript pages until he reached the one of the women crying at the foot of the cross. The mournful looks on their faces reminded him of how Clara had appeared when he'd watched her from across the room, hesitant to interrupt the private moment or to intrude on a sadness he was all too familiar with. While he'd watched her, the anguish and torment he'd suffered after he'd received the Christmas Eve letter six years ago informing him that Lord Matthews had finally agreed to Hugh's requests for his daughter's dowry, and that Hugh and Lady Hermione Matthews's engagement could proceed, had rushed back to him. Along with it had come the regret that had tortured him in the carriage that Christmas morning when he'd ridden away from Stonedown and Clara. The memory of her distraught face when she'd faced him in this very room had torn at him along with the same accusation she'd thrown at him moments ago.

'Fortune hunter. Bollocks.' He slapped the book stand, making it rock before it righted itself. He hadn't married Hermione simply for money, but out of duty to his family. The cold winters at Everburgh when his parents used to struggle to heat even a few rooms while his grandfather had squandered the family fortune on his actress second wife still haunted him, as did the strained and worried faces of his parents. After his grandfather's hard living had finally killed him, the massive debts had fallen to his father to pay and their quality of life, which had never been high, had declined even further. Although his parents had done everything they could to shield Hugh from the reality of their situation, there was nothing their stories of knights and dragons could do to stave off the cold or place more food on the table. Then, when they'd been on the verge of leaving those days behind them for good, Hugh's father's heart had given out, worn down by years of struggles. At his funeral, Hugh had vowed that he would do everything he could to make sure that his mother would one day experience the comfort and ease that a marchioness deserved. His marriage to Hermione had given him the chance to do that and he'd never regretted his decision. He still didn't. It was his youthful indiscretion at not being more cautious with Clara's feelings that he lamented, especially today, but there was nothing he could do to change the past, not his one with her or the last three years. He could only move forward and he would.

Hugh left the library in search of Adam and society, needing both more than solitude and regret. Solitude and the constant torment of remorse had already led him to make too many mistakes in London after Hermione's death, ones he'd have to work twice as hard to overcome if Clara's reaction to him offered any indication of how people currently regarded him. She and they had heard the stories about his behaviour in London. Most of the tales weren't even true, or they were exaggerated far beyond recognition, but it didn't matter. Until recently, he hadn't worked to check them and enough of them were true to give credence to the rest. At one time he'd been admired as much for himself as his old title and had been known to everyone as an honourable and respectable marquess who hadn't inherited his grandfather's taste for ruin. It'd taken a lifetime to build that reputation and three years to throw it all away and make everyone believe he was no better than his grandfather, but he was and he would prove it again.

Striding down the hall, he found Adam in the billiards room with a number of other gentlemen. They bent over the table to examine the shots, change the score on the marker or watch the game, each of them carrying glasses of brandy and sipping them between bits of conversation and breaks in the play. A gaggle of children ran through the room, swarming around the table before running out the opposite door, their noisy chatter barely breaking the conversation of the lords who were willing to tolerate their antics in this season of forgiveness. Hugh hoped everyone was willing to forgive more adult mishaps, especially his.

'Delamare, good to see you.' Adam clapped him on the back, then moved to hand him a glass of brandy from a nearby footman's tray before remembering and setting it back on the salver for someone else to enjoy. 'Sorry, I forgot you'd given it up.'

'There are times when I think that might have been a mistake.' He glanced at the brandy, tempted to throw back a good portion of it and savour the burning in his throat. It was a pain he deserved, but he wasn't a man to go back on his promises, at least not any more.

Adam tilted his head to one side in scrutiny. 'I assume you've seen Clara, then?'

'I have. She wasn't pleased to see me.'

'I'm not surprised.' He didn't look at Hugh, but swirled his brandy in his snifter before taking a generous drink. 'She didn't know you would be here.'

'You didn't tell her?' He wanted to take the snifter and break it over his friend's head. 'The entire reason I wrote to you was so you could warn her in the hopes it might ease any tension between us.' The tension that had dominated every word that had passed between them in the library.

'If I'd told her you'd be here, she wouldn't have come. You know how it is, no one likes to be reminded of past mistakes and such.'

No, they didn't. Not Hugh, not Clara, no one.

'Anyway, it doesn't matter now,' Adam continued. 'You're both here and now you've got your awkward first meeting out of the way, I'm sure the two of you will get on splendidly.'

'I wish I shared your optimism.'

'Well, the season of miracles and all that.' He rapped Hugh on the arm and took up his cue stick and bent over the table to take his shot, the conversation about Clara and Hugh being here together over. Hugh allowed it to drop. Adam was one of the few friends from his past who saw the better in Hugh even when he couldn't see it in himself. Hugh owed it to him to be respectful, especially of Clara. Adam, having inherited young, knew well the responsibilities of a titled man, but for all of his patience and understanding of Hugh's mistakes, and the family duty that had forced him to marry another, Adam would draw the line at intentional injury to those he loved.

'Marvellous shot, Exton,' Lord Tillman muttered through his bushy moustache, one hand on his round belly, the other clutching his brandy. He was tall with spindly legs and long thin arms, his full head of hair a striking contrast to his less-than-robust form. An earl from a long line, he didn't lord his title over anyone, taking it all in stride. He and his wife were two of the most congenial hosts that Hugh had ever known and the most forgiving. Neither of them had baulked at inviting him after he'd placed a gentle request with Lady Tillman when they'd met at the theatre at the end of last Season. He was thankful for their support and this chance to take his first steps towards redeeming himself with good society. If Clara's reaction to him was any gauge, he had a great deal of work to do.

Hugh tried not to sigh in weariness while he watched the game. He intended to some day hold a house party like this at Everburgh, but with no Lady Delamare to help him welcome his guests and no children to run with the guests' children, he would have to live once again off someone else's generosity. It was yet another dream that was on the verge of never coming true, especially if the court ruled against him in the last case concerning Everburgh.

He glanced at the brandy, wanting to knock the drinks to the floor, but he maintained his self-control. He'd done all that duty had required of him when he'd become the Fifth Marquess, paying off the last of the debts with Hermione's money, using Lord Matthew's connections to woo influential lords and hire expensive barristers to settle remaining court cases in his favour or on better terms, but still it hadn't been enough. The estate was in danger once again from a Scottish lord who claimed that Hugh's grandfather had signed over Everburgh to him in exchange for a life annuity and the payment of some debts. The Scotsman had a few letters indicating some sort of deal between him and Hugh's grandfather, and receipts of payment to his grandfather, but he had yet to produce the signed contract. If he did produce it, it would become a matter for a judge to decide. If the court ruled against Hugh, then everything that Hugh, his parents and Hermione had done to save the estate would mean nothing.

Hugh stood up straight and greeted Sir Nathaniel with a hearty welcome, determined to remain polite and solicitous. He would face this unexpected challenge with the fortitude his parents had always shown during their trials, the one he'd demonstrated, too, until Hermione's death had sent him into a dark spiral, but those days were over. He'd made a number of mistakes since Hermione's death, but they and the damage they'd done would soon be behind him. He would enjoy the respect and esteem of these men again, and, if given the opportunity, Clara's, as well. He was the Marquess of Delamare and he would bring dignity to the title and himself once again.

Chapter Two

'My dear, are you sure that's the dress you wish to wear tonight?' Anne asked, entering Clara's room to collect her for dinner. In a short while, everyone would line up according to precedence on the main staircase before going into the dining room. Clara prayed someone had arrived to outrank her, a dowager duchess or a dowager marchioness with an older title than hers who would bump her back a place or two in the line away from Hugh. As much as part of her wanted to be at the head of the line where everyone might see her, she didn't wish to be there beside Hugh.

Given that this wasn't likely to happen, she'd dressed as she would for any other dinner at Lord and Lady Tillman's, careful to pay no special heed to her attire. She didn't wish Hugh to think she'd changed her manner of dress simply because they happened to be beneath the same roof. If Anne's half-frown were any indication, Clara had succeeded a little too well in her desire to under-dress. 'What's wrong with my dress?'

'Nothing, except it's a tad dark.'

'It's winter.' Clara opened her arms and looked down at the black velvet dress devoid of any decoration, trying to sound sensible and failing.

'But the season is so cheerful and you don't want to come across as dour. Perhaps your green dress would be better. You want people to speak with you, not offer consolations.'

Clara dropped her arms in defeat, her desire to be seen as a refined and chic lady fading in the face of her current wardrobe. This dress might be fine and of excellent material but it bore the hallmarks of her grief, as did most of the dresses she'd brought with her. The bright gowns she'd worn before Alfred's death were still packed away in trunks at Winsome Manor. She wished she hadn't left them behind.

'You're right. I appear as if I'm going to a

memorial, not preparing for a festive week. I'll wear the green dress.' She waved for Mary to undo the buttons on the back so Clara could change. 'I don't want to scare whomever I'm paired with for the week's events or give them the impression that they'll be stuck with a stick in the mud.'

'No, you don't.' Anne laid a finger on her cheek, her frown drawing up to one side in a smile that made Clara suspicious. 'Especially since you're sure to be seated beside Lord Delamare.'

'You needn't remind me.' He was the reason she'd already devoted too much time to preparing for dinner. Her inability to find an appropriate dress reminded her of the many times she'd stood before this mirror six years ago, feeling heavy and uncomfortable in all her country finery and inherited jewels, the reflection staring back at her one of a young lady who used to turn down dances for fear that she would step on toes and embarrass herself. Every evening before dinner, she would try on all her dresses, lamenting to Mary about her inability to look like a refined London lady. She'd once thought this was the key to securing Hugh's heart. Instead, the way into his affection had been through more pounds and political influence than her family had possessed.

'I think you should consider yourself very lucky,' Anne said, drawing Clara back to the conversation.

'Lucky? I am far from lucky.' If she were lucky, then Hugh wouldn't be here and she wouldn't feel the need to prove herself to the likes of him or Lady Fulton. She had changed a great deal since the last time she'd been here—now the trick was proving it to everyone else, including herself at times.

'Of course you are. If you forgive him, then there are no barriers to anything happening between the two of you this Christmas.'

Clara gaped at her sister-in-law, unable to believe the words that had just come out of her mouth while Clara was standing in her shift and chemise of all things. Clara stepped into her green dress, yanked it up and stuck her arms in the sleeves. 'Life in the country has become quite dull if you're suggesting something between me and Lord Delamare, a man who is nothing more than a fortune hunter who'd go through my money faster than he does actresses in London.'

'He isn't as bad as you and so many others think,' Anne responded with surprising seriousness, having seen and heard a great deal more of Hugh than Clara had when she'd followed Adam to London every Season. But while she'd been discreet with her tales of him, others had not and a very different picture of him had emerged for Clara.

When Hugh had been a student at the Reverend's school with Adam he hadn't been so bad, but it wasn't the case any more as she sadly knew from experience. During Hugh's many visits to Winsome when she was a girl, he'd seemed so friendly, straightforward and predictable, enjoying riding and hunting like any young gentleman, but the candlelight had never caught in his eyes or his smile been as wide or charming as it had during that Christmas week. Some time between their meeting in the sitting room on the first day and the snowball fight in the garden, Hugh had stopped being simply her elder brother's friend and had become very much more.

It wasn't until the morning that he'd told her he would marry another that he'd suddenly become someone Clara didn't recognise. After that disastrous Christmas, Adam and others had tried to convince her that Hugh wasn't the rake Clara believed him to be. Hugh's behaviour in London had proven them all wrong, making her brother's continued faith in his old friend perplexing. Adam had always had their father's gift of seeing the best in even the worst people. It was a trait she didn't often share and Clara wondered what Hugh hid from Adam and Anne to keep them so enamoured of him. 'What about the duel he fought? Only a true wastrel resorts to that kind of theatrics to resolve a dispute.'

'You know how men are when it comes to their honour. Even the best of them can lose their heads at times.'

'He isn't the best of them, as proven by the tale of him and Miss Palmer at the theatre, the one that was in all the London papers that Lady Bellworth was kind enough to send us as if I'd wanted to hear news of Hugh, good or bad.'

'According to Adam, the story is quite overblown. I think once you speak with him at dinner you'll see that he isn't the rake those rumours make him out to be.'

'I doubt it.' Clara peered at Anne while Mary did up the back buttons, amazed, after her earlier show of concern downstairs, that she would be this cavalier about Clara and Hugh. 'Even if he is, I don't care. I learned the hard way about him once before. It's all I need to know about his character.'

She viewed herself in the mirror, silently admitting that the green dress did suit her better. Good. It would make her diamond and emerald necklace stand out and help banish the old self-consciousness nipping at her. While Hugh's rejection had wounded her burgeoning confidence years ago, Alfred had made her certain of it, but he was gone and it was up to her to maintain her belief in herself.

She glanced at the door to her room and at the shiny knob reflecting the firelight. Just on the other side of it was where she and Alfred had truly met for the first time, on that Christmas morning after she'd come upstairs from meeting Hugh for the last time.

She'd struggled to remain composed until she'd been able to reach this side of the door and cry, but Alfred had been there to help soothe her broken heart…

'Lady Exton, are you well?'

Genuine concern and not just the nicety of manners had driven Lord Kingston's question. It had been there in his blue eyes with their faint lines at the corners.

He was older than her—thirty-five, perhaps—with dark hair touched with grey at the temples and the regal air of his class. He stood straight and tall, his strong features making him more debonair than a man like Lord Westbook, but there was a kindness about him that called to Clara.

'Since the passing of my parents I sometimes find the holidays difficult to endure.'

If she'd known him better she might have wailed on his shoulder, as she wished she could still do with her mother who would have rushed to comfort her. But her mother was no longer there to offer her love or wisdom or even the strength to face the other guests.

All day today she'd have to sit beside everyone in church and across the table at dinner and pretend to be cheerful while her heart continued to break. Everyone had seen her and Hugh walking and playing cards and spending almost every moment they could in one another's company. His having left and her looking more like it was All Hallows' Eve than Christmas morning would make it obvious to everyone what had happened.

Hugh hadn't just trifled with her and jilted her, he'd done it in the most public way imaginable, making the pain even more deep.

'I understand. It was a great many years before I could enjoy Christmas after my wife passed. I assure you, Lady Exton, it does get easier with time.'

'Does it?' she whispered.

Her mother would have seen Hugh for the fortune hunter he really was and she would have warned Clara off him as she had the other fortune hunters in London. The lack of her mother's love and guidance further tarnished an already clouded morning.

He reached into the pocket of his coat and took out a white handkerchief and handed it to her. 'It does.'

She took his handkerchief and dabbed at her eyes, embarrassed for almost losing her poise. 'I'm sorry to cast a shadow over the merry day.'

'Don't be. A pretty young lady like you is allowed to be sad from time to time. If you weren't, one would think you didn't have a heart. May I escort you down to breakfast?'

He'd held out his arm to her, the tenderness in his eyes difficult to abandon for the cold emptiness of her room. There'd been enough of those sorts of mornings in the last two years, between her father's death and then her mother's passing. That Christmas had been supposed to be better—and it had been until that morning.

It could be again. She refused to make a pitying spectacle of herself in front of the other guests. Here was a man offering her genuine regard when she needed it, there was no reason not to accept.

She slid her hand over his arm and stood confidently beside him. 'Yes, Lord Kingston, you may.'

The clang of the gong echoed up from the main hall and pulled her away from the sweet memory and back into the reality of the present. It was time to go down for dinner and

Alfred wasn't here to walk with her tonight. She must face whatever awaited her alone and deal with it as best she could. It made her wish she had packed up and gone back to Winsome.

No. I won't be so weak. She took the gloves that Mary held out to her, cursing the tremor in her hands while she tugged them on. She shouldn't be this nervous. Hugh meant nothing to her and what had happened was a long time ago. Except he did mean something, he represented everything Clara had been before she'd become a marchioness, an ill-at-ease girl who, despite a respectable inheritance, had been unable to catch or hold a gentleman's attention long enough to secure a proposal. She was no longer that woman, but echoes of that girl dogged her steps as she escorted Anne out of her room and down the hall towards the stairs.

The old awkwardness was especially potent when they spied the end of the line of people waiting to queue up for dinner. A number of them smiled and nodded appreciatively, but it wasn't them that Clara fixed on, but Lord Westbook and Lady Fulton. They stood one step apart, with Lord Fulton too engrossed in conversation with Lord Worth above him to care if his wife spent her time whispering to Lord Westbook. Lady Fulton's small eyes widened at the sight of Clara, and Lord Westbook stopped his incessant talking to take Clara in.

Clara's awkwardness melted away and she held her head high and strode forward with purpose, thankful Anne had suggested she change. Clara hadn't forgotten Lady Fulton's derisive remarks about her six years ago and the way they'd revealed her true opinion of Clara. She was not a girl in a simple dress and wearing her jewellery as if it were nothing better than an old chandelier chain that she'd decided to drape around her neck. Clara's gown might be muted, but it was fine, and the emeralds she wore spoke of her increased status. She was no longer a plain country mouse, but a refined lady.

'Lady Kingston, there you are. Come now, you must take your place beside Lord Delamare so we may all go in,' Lady Tillman called out, moving up through the parting guests to reach Clara and take her by the hand.

Clara did her best to concentrate on the

stairs and not trip over Lady Tillman's short train as her hostess pulled her down the stairs. Around her, the line had gone silent and she could almost hear people wondering if they would be treated to the same show of courting and rejection that they'd witnessed six years ago. They would not enjoy any sort of amusement from her, assuming Hugh decided to behave with dignity when she reached him. If he wished to give a little of what he'd got from her in the library, this was a perfect opportunity to do it. She didn't think him so petty, but after what she'd heard of him in London, it was a possibility. It made her want to twist out of Lady Tillman's grip and run back to her room, but she would not look like a coward in front of the other guests, especially Lady Fulton. Instead, she would sit next to Hugh at dinner with all the bearing and dignity of a marchioness and everyone else could get their entertainment elsewhere.

Lady Tillman and Clara finally reached the bottom of the stairs and Clara stopped before Hugh, her heart racing from both the quick descent and her nerves. If Clara's attire had changed in six years, then so had

Hugh's. He was taller than the gentlemen on the step above him and his broad shoulders did more credit to the wool covering them than the talents of his Jermyn Street tailor. His dark trousers hugged his trim middle and thighs, and he wore his hair combed back off his strong face, the knot of his white cravat tucked neatly beneath his square chin. If she hadn't heard the rumours, she would have thought he'd spent the last three years at Everburgh riding and engaging in other sports, not in debauchery at the theatres and clubs of London.

'Good evening, Lord Delamare,' she greeted, trying to convince everyone, including herself, that it made no difference to her if she was seated next to him and that she could be gracious and friendly to an old flame with the poise expected of a woman of her standing.

'Good evening, Lady Kingston. You look lovely tonight.' His unstudied words raised Clara's confidence higher than when she'd approached Lady Fulton at the top of the stairs and allowed her to breathe again. She hadn't known what to expect when she'd descended, but she hadn't expected this compliment and it almost rattled her surety, especially when Lady Tillman laid Clara's hand on Hugh's arm.

The sight of her satin-covered fingers against the black fabric of his coat brought back a hundred memories. They were of Alfred escorting her into dinner or a ballroom, the two of them chatting and laughing while they walked. It'd been two years since she'd stood beside a man like this and loneliness and loss overwhelmed her. It should be Alfred beside her, but it wasn't and it never would be again.

'Are you all right, Lady Kingston?' Hugh laid his hand comfortingly over hers.

She raised her face to his, having forgotten for a moment to keep her chin up. She offered him a weak smile, trying to be regain her composure, but it was difficult with his warm hand covering hers. If she could let down her guard long enough to tell him the truth, she would, but she couldn't, not here and certainly not with him. 'Yes, only sometimes I find it difficult at this time of year.'

It was the most she could say.

'I understand.' He squeezed her fingers, his thumb lightly brushing hers, the steady motion soothing her. There was nothing calculated in the gesture or his words, only a desire to ease her pain in a way very few had tried to do since the weeks surrounding the funeral.

'Are you ready to lead them in?' Lady Tillman asked, drawing Clara's attention away from Hugh.

'Yes, of course,' Clara stammered, everything she'd intended to do tonight from walking regally like a queen to ignoring Hugh thrown into confusion. For a long time, her grief had been hers alone to bear, expected by all to grow fainter as time passed, but he'd seen it and for a moment he'd helped her to shoulder it. This was a greater comfort to her than all the showing up of Lady Fulton and Lord Westbook, and it stunned her that it should come from him. After the way she'd spoken to him in the library, she'd expected derision instead of kindness.

They started off down the hall and she raised her head high, concentrating on the pearls woven in their hostess's coiffure and not Hugh's steady steps or the shift of his arm beneath her palm. His hand remained covering hers, the pressure of his fingers distracting. She wished he'd acted like a rake instead of a gentleman. It would make it so much easier to decide how to behave with him tonight. While his kind words were appreciated, it didn't change their past or her opinion of him and this unfortunate seating arrangement.

They all strolled into the dining room. The table was bereft of treats and laid out in its splendid china and silver which glistened in the high polish of the table's finish. Everything about this room was sumptuous with the walls done in a deep red wallpaper covered with numerous gilded frames of hunting portraits and the English countryside. Along the edges of the room, the guests moved past fine burled oak sideboards with marble tops and elaborate candelabras, vases and other adornments. At the other end, a large fire roared in a hearth decorated by white moulding similar in shape to the classical front of Stonedown Manor. Clara pitied Lord Tillman who would sit with his back to the blaze and likely roast as much as the meat course. If he did mind the heat, he never said anything, enduring it so the guests at Clara's end of the table would not shiver through the meal.

Despite the formality of the setting, everyone except those newest to the party approached their seats in leisure as if they were in their own homes. When they reached their places, Hugh finally let go of Clara and she took her place beside Lady Tillman, conscious of every move Hugh made when he sat down on her right. With Lord Worth on Lady Tillman's other side and dominating her attention with conversation, Clara realised she would either have to slurp her soup in silence or find a way to speak with Hugh. She didn't wish to converse with him at all, but to be alone and think about what had just happened. He hadn't behaved at all as she'd expected and she'd been foolish enough to allow a touch of kindness to make her almost slip and reveal to him something of the lonely woman beneath the confident Marchioness. He didn't deserve to see that woman or to know the details of her heart, both good and bad. He deserved nothing but her disdain, but it was difficult to find the resolve to deride him so severely again.

Unable to decide what to do, she did nothing except remain silent and listen to the conversations around her while she ate. Hugh was in no hurry to break the stalemate either. Where he'd been quite free with his words in the library and then again on the stairs, he'd gone mute now, focusing on his plate as if it was the most important thing in the room. He didn't even make an effort to speak to Lady Pariston who sat on his other side. The manners her mother had instilled in her urged Clara to at least mention the weather, but she couldn't bring herself to do even that. She didn't want to appear like an overeager debutante and force him into a conversation he clearly didn't want. Instead, she continued to eat her soup, thankful that with the balls and other events, there wouldn't be too many similar dinners to endure this week.

Clara swirled her soup with her spoon, leaving a quickly disappearing trail in the thick, pale green surface, the tension between them ruining the taste of her food. This was not at all how she'd imagined this week unfolding and she wondered, if she chose to go with Anne and Adam to London, if that experience would be any better. There had been moments of delight during her first Season in London, but they'd quickly faded while she'd stood against the wall at dances or watched her mother send yet another young man with a pile of debts in search of a rich wife packing. Returning to London as the wife of a peer in the House of Lords had been so much better. She'd been proud of Alfred's accomplishments and had done her best to help him by hosting dinners for his political friends and attending balls. She hadn't returned to town since his death, not wanting to face all its pitfalls alone. She would have to face it if she wanted to find a new life, for the society of the country was very limited if Hugh's presence was any indication. Lady Tillman must be hard up for guests to have invited him.

She glanced past Hugh to thin Lady Pariston with her lace shawl and tweedy-coloured dress, the weight of the large diamond necklace she wore making her hunched posture more pronounced. While Clara used to enjoy sitting with Lady Pariston by the fire in the evenings and listening to her tales of Stonedown Manner in the old days, she wondered if becoming a similar little old lady was to be her fate. She was a dowager, too, and glancing around the table, it was clear there would be no Alfred to rescue her this time from an ignoble future. It made her lose her appetite.

Then she caught Hugh's gaze and her heart made a little flutter. No, he wouldn't rescue her either, unless he deemed her purse large enough to make her more attractive. It would be up to her to find some other way of moving on long after this party concluded, but, touching her gloved hand to where the imprint of Hugh's heaviness still lingered, it was difficult not to remember a previous Christmas that had been full of potential, until it hadn't been.

Hugh set down his soup spoon and sat back against the chair, allowing the footman to take away the half-eaten dish and replace it with the next course. Beside him, Clara began to eat her fish, her gloved hand moving the silver fork elegantly back and forth from the plate to her full red lips. Every now and then she'd lean forward in her seat, lengthening the line of her back, her pert chin pressed out a touch above the long line of her neck to where it curved down to her supple chest. The whiteness of her skin was a stark contrast to the deep green of her gown. The colour matched the richness of the emeralds in her necklace and the jewels sparkled with each of her movements. The cut of her bodice, although modest, still revealed a touch of the soft creaminess of her chest. She was finely attired even if it whispered of mourning, but the heavier material flattered her more than the wispy gowns of the women who'd come up from London for the house party. The gown added grace to her once-awkward movements and told him that she had grown a great deal since the last time he'd seen her.

She set down her fork and frowned a touch when she could not catch all the words of Lord Worth's conversation with Lady Missington from across the table. That Clara longed to be sitting next to him and taking in every story about the last session of Parliament instead of beside Hugh was clear. If it were in his power to release her to do so, he would, but they sat where precedence dictated and they were beholden to it, and to each other to make conversation, except they had yet to make any.

Hugh poked at his fish and the white sauce covering it. He'd spoken to Clara twice today.

The first time, she'd sneered at him and his reputation and accused him of being in search of money, leaving him in no doubt about her opinion of him. The next time, with her standing beside him, her hair swept off her neck and done in ringlets at the back of her head that shivered with each of her delicate movements, she'd lost her sneer and the veil of courage she'd worn when she'd descended the stairs to reveal the grieving woman beneath. Without thinking, he'd laid his hand on hers, recognising her hurt and longing to crush it like a walnut shell. She didn't deserve to suffer, but to enjoy her youth and the merry season. He'd succeeded for a quick moment in easing a pain he knew all too well, but his comfort hadn't lasted. Nor had it been enough to change her mind about him, even a little. She remained determined to think the worst of him and make him endure her silence because of it.

He cast Clara another sideways glance and she paused in her eating, conscious of his scrutiny and quickly meeting his curious gaze before she returned to her fish. He let her go, but not without a great deal of guilt. He'd ruined her Christmas once before by being too open and easy with her when he should have been more guarded and reserved, reminding him of how much she'd changed since they'd last sat at this table together. Back then, she'd been further down the line of precedence and across from him, hindering any chance he might have had to speak with her despite their eagerness to converse. They'd spoken instead through longing glances, smiles and coquettish looks tossed across the table, not careful or caring if anyone else saw them, and it had increased her embarrassment in the end.

People would whisper again, but this time it would be about the stony silence between them, the one that had already garnered a number of small frowns from Lady Exton from where she sat next to her husband. Once in a while she would comment to Adam who would glance up at Clara and Hugh. He didn't silently urge Hugh to speak to his sister, but simply offered a few words to his wife before returning to his meal. Hugh set down his fork and picked up the punch he'd requested from the footman. The sweetness nearly made him gag. His failed courtship of Clara had almost cost him his friendship with Adam, he didn't wish to risk it again by mistaking the brief moment at the bottom of the stairs for something more than a genuine thank you for his having been kind. This silence was intolerable, but he would endure it to keep the peace between himself and Adam and to spare Clara from any derision that his previous lack of discretion had caused her. He had no one but himself to blame for her poor opinion of him and again he cursed his actions of the last three years.

Hugh took in the other guests who were too engaged in discussion with those around them to notice him, but he caught a few curious looks thrown in his direction now and then. It was clear in the way that many regarded him with sidelong glances that they'd heard the stories about him and continued to wonder if they were true. He would show them they weren't through his actions and defy all their low expectations, even Clara's. He was here to begin the slow process of undoing his mistakes in London after Hermione's death, to rebuild the good name he'd once prided himself on holding, the one he'd carelessly tossed away in his grief. No whiff of scandal could touch him, especially while

Lord Westbook was here and no doubt watching for any more stories to entertain other hostesses with. Everything Hugh did this week, especially in regards to Clara, must be above board and if it meant sitting here in silence beside Clara until she chose to break it, then so be it. He'd endured worse things in his duty to the Delamare name. He could endure this even while he wished there was some way he could change it.

At the end of the meal, Lady Tillman led the ladies out of the room while Lord Tillman called for the brandy. The men rose from their places of precedent and took up more informal seats at Lord Tillman's end of the table. Hugh chose the chair beside Sir Nathaniel, eager to talk to the man who, before his ennoblement, had been a celebrated barrister and who understood the vagaries of the law better than most titled men. The letter informing Hugh that a lawsuit for possession of Everburgh had been filed had forced him out of London as much as his disgust with himself. He might have turned away from duty and responsibility for a while, but he hadn't given up on it entirely because it wasn't an easy thing to set aside, nor could he abandon trying to accomplish everything that his father and even Hermione had sacrificed their lives to help him achieve. It might mean more struggle and difficulties, but he would see this through and seize every advantage available to him, including setting his pride aside and asking for help from Sir Nathaniel, Lord Tillman and Adam.

To Hugh's dismay, Lord Westbook took the chair on Hugh's opposite side. He gave the man no notice as he leaned in towards Sir Nathaniel. 'I understand you once handled a case concerning the signing over of an estate when the signee was in no position to make such a decision and succeeded in having the contract voided.'

'I did.' Sir Nathaniel leaned forward with his elbows against the table to give them some privacy in their discussion. The rest of the gentlemen sat back, savouring their drinks and the conversation, while Lord Westbook sat ramrod straight in his chair, no doubt watching and listening to everything. Let him hear what Sir Nathaniel had to say, his opinion and all his stupid little stories meant nothing to Hugh. Besides, the pending case was already well known in London and another of the many tales already attached to his name. 'And I'm familiar with your case.'

'What do you think of it?'

'I think you have a solid one against the enforcement of the contract, should the Scotsman ever produce it. Who's representing you?'

'No one, yet.' He couldn't afford any long, drawn-out payments to solicitors. Everburgh might be clear of debts, but the harvest had not sufficiently recovered enough to provide a robust income. Hugh must continue to economise and endure a few more lean years before he and his estate workers could at last breathe easy, assuming Everburgh wasn't stolen out from under him. 'I was thinking of engaging Featherton and Associates.'

'A good firm, but not the one for something like this. You need Allenton and Associates, one of their best barristers used to work for me, I trained him up. He knows the case you're referring to and has handled other matters dealing with questionable contacts. He's the best for you.'

And expensive, Hugh thought, but in a matter like this he could not afford to be stingy.

He would find a way to obtain the money to pay for their services, he had no choice. 'I'll be certain to engage them.'

The footman tried to set a snifter of brandy before Hugh, but he waved it away.

'Is there another spirit I can offer you, Lord Delamare?' the footman asked, eager like his employer to make the guests happy.

'None, thank you.'

'Nothing to warm the soul on a cold night?' Sir Nathaniel asked, taking up his drink.

'I warmed my soul one too many times on both cold and hot nights to realise I need to return to simpler more noble pursuits, such as my estate.'

'An admirable choice a number of gentlemen would do well to make.' Sir Nathaniel regarded him with an appraising look, the kind Hugh usually saw in mamas sizing him up at balls as a potential catch before they wrinkled their noses in displeasure and moved on to greener and less tarnished pastures. Hugh waited for Sir Nathaniel to do the same, but instead he took a deep sip of his drink and set it down, more admiration in his expression than reprimand.

'If you'd like, I can write to Allenton and

Associates to recommend you to them so you receive their best service,' Sir Nathaniel offered.

'I'd like that very much.' This raised his spirits more than brandy ever could. This was not the usual reaction he received from those who'd appraised him of late, especially those with whom he was not well acquainted. There was no reason for Sir Nathaniel to assist him, but Hugh was glad of his kindness and generosity and would do all he could to deserve it.

It was then Lord Westbook sat forward, his long and narrow face punctuated by a too snake-like smile. 'I'm sure your turn towards temperance in this and other pursuits will help you a great deal in your case, Lord Delamare.'

Hugh pinned the man with a hard stare, in no mood to share any of his personal matters with this weasel. 'My behaviour has no bearing on the enforcement of the law.'

'Behaviour always has a bearing on cases for judges are men like any other and, given your opponent's spotless reputation, a judge might look upon him more favourably than he does you.'

'Careful how you call my reputation into question, Lord Westbook, or I may find a way to revive it in your eyes with a more formal challenge,' Hugh growled in a low voice. Thankfully, Mr Alton asked Sir Nathaniel a question, drawing his attention away from the less-than-civil turn in Hugh and Lord Westbook's conversation.

Lord Westbook went pale beneath his ruddy complexion, his spine not so stiff when faced with a challenge more formidable than making society ladies titter with delight at scandalous tales in order to secure an invitation to yet another party.

Hugh rather hoped Lord Westbook was man enough to force his hand, but Hugh didn't wish to be rude to their host or to lose Sir Nathaniel's newfound respect by calling out a fellow guest. Nor did he appreciate the kernel of truth in Lord Westbook's nasty words. Hugh might not have done more than most lords in London, but he'd been careless in keeping it discreet. Lord Westbook was right. If his matter came before the wrong judge, Hugh's past behaviour might be taken into account. It made his need to be impeccable and avoid any whiff of scandal from here on out far more pressing.

'Lady Kingston, we haven't had a chance to speak since you arrived.' Lady Fulton squeezed in between Clara and Lady Pariston where they sat on the sofa, enjoying the fire and a great deal of catching up. Anne had been forced to leave the women directly after dinner to help take care of poor Lillie who'd eaten too many sweets and become sick in the nursery where the rest of the children dined. From across the new arrival, Lady Pariston threw Clara a sympathetic and curious look, both of them wondering what in the world Lady Fulton could possibly have to speak with Clara about. Lord Fulton was an agreeable man, but his considerably younger wife, who'd possessed more mercantile money than lineage before becoming Lady Fulton, wasn't such a charming delight. She was tall and slender, and although her bloom had faded she was still attractive. However, her constant sneer did a great deal to temper it. 'I must say, your necklace is gorgeous. Was it your mother's?'

'No, it was a Christmas present from my

late husband,' Clara answered coolly, irked by the woman's uninvited intrusion and her ignoring Lady Pariston.

'He had exquisite taste in jewellery,' she purred with a covetousness to make Clara think she meant Alfred had more taste in baubles than he did ladies, but she smiled and accepted the compliment with far more graciousness than Lady Fulton deserved. 'It's a pity precedence has forced you to waste this display of finery on a man like Lord Delamare. One would think after what happened the last time the two of you were here together that he would have had the decency to stay away. I'm surprised, given his reputation in town, that he was even invited.' She raised her hand to speak from the back of it as if she and Clara were sharing some great intimacy. 'As much as I adore Lady Tillman, I've always questioned her selection of guests. Sometimes they can be so common.'

Her gaze flicked over Clara, who was certain that Lady Fulton was including her in that collection. Clara's title might garner her respect, but not from everyone, especially someone like Lady Fulton who, despite the fashionableness of her dark blue evening dress, and the gaudy gold jewellery she wore, could not completely hide her more humble roots.

'I believe a wide variety of guests always lends a touch of surprise to any gathering. One never knows who one might meet here, isn't that right, Lady Pariston?'

'It is,' the grand dame concurred, too old to be ruffled by a parvenu like Lady Fulton. 'Who knows what might come of new friendships.'

'But they aren't all new, are they?' Lady Fulton leaned closer to Clara, her look of affected concern as sickening as her overly sweet perfume. 'It can't be easy for you to see him again.'

Clara sat up straighter so she could peer down her nose at the rude woman. Whatever impression she'd made on Lady Fulton in the hallway before dinner had worn off. It was time to assert herself again. 'I find it as easy to see him as I do to see those who overstep the bounds of propriety by speaking too intimately to their betters.'

Lady Fulton jerked back and pressed her thin lips tight together at having been put in her place and by Clara of all people. Clearly she hadn't expected this show of spirit and if she hadn't risen at that moment to seek out other companionship, she would have tasted a great deal more of it. Clara almost wished she had stayed for, with her hackles raised and the tension still lingering from dinner, a little tiff would help her sit much easier on the sofa while they waited for the men to join them.

'Well done, Lady Kingston,' Lady Pariston congratulated, patting her on the knee. 'You stood up to her as you should.'

'I wish it hadn't been necessary to do so.' But Lady Fulton had been the one to strike the first blow. Who was she to cast any aspersions on Clara or even Hugh? Yet she'd felt bold enough to do it simply because of Hugh's presence and their unfortunate seating at the dinner table. 'With any luck, that will put an end to any of her other observations about me, at least in public.'

She could not control what they said in private any more than she could command Hugh to leave. She could only hope that nothing else happened this weekend to give that vile woman or anyone else more cause to look down their noses at her or to insist on seeing her as nothing more than the awkward young girl she'd once been. She would not be made to feel inconsequential again, not by Lady Fulton and certainly not by Hugh.

'Care less what others think and you'll be happier, I promise,' Lady Pariston instructed, as if able to hear her doubts about herself and this week. 'Besides, the way Lord Delamare regarded you tonight won't silence anyone's tongues and if they're going to whisper then you might as well give them something worth whispering about. A house party is as good a place as any to do it.'

'Lady Pariston!' Clara could not believe she was having this conversation with a woman who could be her grandmother or that Lady Pariston was suggesting that Hugh had regarded her with a great deal of interest. The only thing he was probably interested in was her money.

'Oh, don't look so shocked. You'd be surprised by what all these ladies get up to, but you won't hear about it because they're discreet. I was discreet, too, and oh, I did have my fun, not when I was married, mind you, but on a number of occasions afterwards.' She laid a wrinkled and bejewelled hand on her chest and smiled with winsome pride.

'With a little discretion you could get up to a little trouble with that fine specimen of a marquess yourself.'

First Anne, now Lady Pariston. There were times when Clara seemed like the only one who cared about the blemishes of Hugh's past. 'I've already had enough trouble with Lord Delamare and, judging by what I've heard of him, he's had a fair amount of his own trouble.'

'Good, it means he knows his way around a woman.' Lady Pariston winked at her before throwing back her head and laughing. Clara's cheeks began to burn as people turned to view them before returning to their amusement. Then Lady Pariston sobered and faced her again. 'Seriously, my dear, you have been placed in this position at far too young an age and now you must make the best of it. Don't work so hard to please others, only yourself, and if that pleasure should include the young man, then so be it.'

Clara waved her hand in front of her face against the heat of the fire. 'I assure you, what I want does not include Lord Delamare.'

'Don't be so set against it. It does no good for a woman to be alone, especially when there is a man willing to keep her company.' Lady Pariston sat back, regarding her out of the corner of her eyes as if she didn't believe for a moment what Clara had said.

Clara laid her hand in her lap with a sigh. She could insist it was true but there was no point. Lady Pariston was right, people would believe what they wanted and Clara should not be guided by a desire to try to control it. All she could control was how she responded to everyone, including Hugh, but she had no energy to do any more of that tonight. Rising, she offered the ladies goodnight and took her leave, unwilling to wait for the arrival of the men.

It would be a pleasure to be alone in her room where no one expected more of her than blowing out her candle before she fell asleep and she didn't need to deal with the issue of Hugh and how to handle him while she was here. She wasn't about to follow Lady Pariston's advice, but she was at a loss for her own ideas about what to do. She needed her rest if she was going to face more of it tomorrow. Heaven knew this was not how she'd expected this week to be.

Chapter Three

'You and Lord Delamare were quite silent at dinner last night,' Anne remarked, taking the empty seat beside Clara in the sitting room where all the guests were gathering for the traditional partnering for the week's activities. The ladies wore their sturdy pelisses and shoes and held their leather gloves in anticipation of an outside game. The weather had remained pleasant if not cold and everyone was sure the Tillmans would take advantage of it to amuse their guests. The men were equally bundled up in heavier coats and redingotes, but everyone had undone the top few buttons to keep from sweltering in the warm sitting room.

'We weren't completely silent,' Clara explained matter of factly. 'I asked him to pass the salt and he was most obliging.'

'Yes, quite the conversation.' Anne rolled her eyes.

'I wonder who we'll be paired with,' Clara mused, eager to change the subject as she glanced around at the motley collection of titled and untitled guests scattered about the room. She rather hoped it would be with eighteen-year-old Lord Wortley so she could help set him at ease. She remembered what it was like to be without one's parents at his age and how awkward it'd been. Thankfully, Hugh wasn't here. With any luck he would continue to stay away and she would be spared his presence for the better part of the day. Sadly, there was still tonight's dinner to endure.

'I'm sure it will be exciting no matter who is chosen for you.'

'I hope so.' The festive activities here had always been one of Clara's favourite parts of the annual house party.

Lord Tillman sat in an armchair next to the fireplace, entertaining James, Lillie and a number of other children with a sleight-of-hand card trick. If Lord Tillman weren't such an honourable and forthright gentleman, he could make a great deal of money at the tables with such tricks, but, recognising his talent, he often refused to play unless it was for fun or small stakes. He would make the cards disappear as if by magic, eliciting from the children oohs of amazement before he made the card reappear from behind one of their ears, sending the children into fits of laughter. Their delight both warmed and saddened Clara. There wasn't a child of hers among them to marvel at Lord Tillman's sleight of hand.

The curtain of melancholy threatened to fall over her again, but its descent was halted by the arrival of Hugh. With him standing on the threshold taking in the guests before his attention alighted on her, the last thing she wanted was to appear glum or to risk losing a single tear. He'd humiliated her enough in front of most of these people once before. She didn't need her private sorrows, no matter how much they seared her heart, leaving her in a crying puddle to be pitied. Determined to appear at ease, she touched the combs in the back of her coiffure, pretending as if Hugh's arrival made no difference to her.

He soon looked away from her and strode up to Sir Nathaniel and began to chat with him. As if aware that she was watching him, he tossed her a quick glance that made her drop her gaze to her feet and the sturdy boots she wore. She wasn't sure how long he regarded her, but no matter where she looked or how much she concentrated on the view through the window she could not forget that he stood only the length of the room away from her. Outside, the snow that had threatened yesterday had not fallen, but the clouds lingered to blot out the sunshine and cast a grey pall over the countryside. Very soon, or so everyone had discussed at breakfast, they expected to see snow. It would be a great delight for the children and the guests since the Tillmans owned a sleigh that they placed at their guests' disposal for rides. Clara and Hugh had taken advantage of the Tillmans' generosity with the sleigh many times during their last visit, with Hugh expertly handling the ribbons as he'd guided the sturdy plough horse over the gently sloping hills and wide fields. Clara would sit close beside him, her hips pressed against his and the lap blanket spread across both their thighs to keep them warm. During the rides, he'd talked endlessly about his hopes for Everburgh and how his inheritance sat heavy on his shoulders. He'd explained to her all his ideas for improving the manor lands to increase the crops and the profits derived from them, and she'd encouraged every one of them, convinced that he would succeed in making Everburgh as magnificent as it had once been. As she'd held tight to his arm, sometimes leaning her head on his shoulder, she'd imaged herself beside him, helping him overcome all the difficulties that he'd endured over the years until they were firmly set in the past. Clara had understood what it was like to struggle under the weight of a title for she'd watched Adam assume the earldom and all responsibility for Winsome after their father had died. She knew how difficult it was to make the transition and how much more so it was for Hugh. Winsome had been well managed and smoothly run with nothing like the troubles that had plagued Everburgh. While Hugh had spoken, the breath of the horses driving the sleigh had risen like clouds over their heads and Clara had dreamed of helping him make his dreams for the manor come true.

Clara flicked a piece of fluff off the skirt of her pelisse, missing that old easiness with Hugh. There'd been none of it last night and when she turned from the window and her eyes caught his again, all the stiff awkwardness returned. Not even when Hugh had been nothing more than Adam's friend and she a pest of a little sister had his mere presence in the same house as her been so unpleasant. At least back then, when they were little more than children, he'd held some genuine regard for her.

'Don't stare too much, Clara, or people will talk,' Anne teasingly warned.

'I wasn't staring, I was simply marvelling at how well he conceals the meaner side of his personality.' He'd hidden it from Clara, her parents and even Adam, so much so, her brother still pretended these traits didn't exist. Adam approached Hugh who offered her brother the first smile she'd seen since his arrival, even if it was a shallow one that faded fast. She wished she could be so at ease with him.

'It isn't as mean as you wish to believe. He was grieving, Clara, like you and chose to deal with it in his own way,' Anne insisted, but Clara wasn't convinced.

'By acting like his grandfather and dallying with half the actresses in London?'

'Lord Delamare isn't the awful man you think he is and if you simply spoke to him I think you would see that.'

Clara wondered at Anne's continued defence of the man and if Anne knew something about Hugh's situation that Clara was not privy to, but there was no time to ask for Lady Tillman entered the room carrying an old hat. A ripple of excitement spread through the still as she joined Lord Tillman at the fireplace.

'Welcome, everyone, and thank you so much for joining us again. It warms the heart to have my family and all my old friends and their children near at this special time of year,' Lady Tillman announced.

'Hear, hear.' A rousing cheer went up from the men while the women offered polite applause. The children were shooed out of the room by their nurses and governesses while Lord Tillman explained about the hat and the pairing for those new to the group. Lady Tillman would draw a woman's name from her hat and then Lord Tillman would draw a man's name from his hat. Those two people would then be paired together for each activity that Lord and Lady Tillman had devised for the week. It was one of the rituals that had been taking place here for so many years and would, if fate allowed, continue for many more to come.

When at last the Tillmans were done thanking and welcoming and explaining, a footman came forward to hold the two hats. Lady Tillman drew the first lady's name.

'Lady Pariston.'

The Dowager nodded from where she sat wrapped in a large shawl.

Lord Tillman reached his hand into his hat and pulled out a name. 'Lord Wortley.'

The room applauded the strange pairing, while Lord Wortley rose to join his new partner. Clara almost slumped her shoulders in disappointment before the announcement of the next pairing drew her back into the excitement of the morning, one tinged with a touch of anxiety at Hugh's continued presence. She did her best to ignore it and to enjoy instead the anticipation and laughter that met each new announced pair. Family members and strangers were brought together or separated in the spirit of the Christmas festivities and Clara waited, wondering who she would end up with for a partner when at last Lady Tillman drew out her name.

'Lady Kingston,' she announced.

'And what lucky man will be paired with what I can only describe as the loveliest of ladies and the most eligible?' Lord Tillman teased while he dipped his hand into the hat and rustled the paper. Then at last he drew out a small slip and opened it. Clara balled her hands over her legs and waited as if she were receiving a Christmas morning present.

Lord Tillman's eyebrows rose a touch before he showed the slip to his wife, who giggled like a young girl before the both of them turned to face Clara.

Lord Tillman's clear voice rang out. 'Lord Delamare.'

Clara nearly fell out of her chair. No, no, no, this wasn't possible.

A quick intake of surprise almost sucked the smoke from the chimney as all eyes turned to either her or Hugh. Both Clara and Hugh knew what was expected of them, they should rise and, in a fit of laughter and smiles, pair up on a sofa or in the matched chairs near the window, but neither of them moved. Clara didn't so much as look at him as she struggled to smile, to breathe, to do anything except sit there like a startled rabbit.

It was Anne who broke the ice, clapping and laughing as was expected of the guests after each announcement. Slowly, the rest of the room joined in. Clara shot Anne a stiff smile, hoping her sister-in-law would catch the panic just beneath. She had no desire to be paired with Hugh for dinner much less for every activity of the entire week, but it was either speak up and insist that Lord Tillman draw again and be rude to their host and cause even more unnecessary whispering or rise and take her place beside Hugh. Not wishing to make more of a spectacle of herself than she feared she already was, she had no choice but to get up and join him.

Why in heaven's name had she allowed Anne to talk her into coming to this house party?

Clara stood slowly, putting on her best party face as she turned to greet Hugh in the centre of the room. He wore a similarly false and overly wide smile, pretending like her that this was not a very unexpected and unwanted turn of events. Her heart raced, not with excitement like it had six years ago, but with the painful realisation that everyone was watching them. Not even Lord and Lady Tillman had moved on to form the next couple—they, like the rest of their guests, were waiting for Hugh and Clara to move aside. Not one to prolong the awkward moment, Clara made for an open seat near the window and Hugh followed her. They said nothing about the imposed partnership, but sat through the rest of the pairings, clapping as stiffly at each announcement as they had during the four words they'd exchanged at dinner last night.

Adam and Anne, by chance again, were paired up to their mutual delight while Lord Westbook found himself with Lady Fulton. Lord Fulton was left to join with Lady Worth while Sir Nathaniel was paired with Mrs Alton. Clara thought Lord Westbook and Lady Fulton a good match for they were both overly fond of gossip and would have a great deal to discuss while they were together, unlike she and Hugh. Heaven knew what catty remarks that pair of busybodies would make about Clara this time.

No, I shouldn't care. Lady Pariston's suggestion to ignore people's whispering came back to her, but Clara found it difficult to shrug off her concern. She didn't like being the subject of gossip, good or bad, and here she was at the centre of it again and it was all Hugh's fault.

Finally, the pairing complete, Lord and Lady Tillman had the footman take away the hats and set to explaining the first activity.

'It's a scavenger hunt,' Lady Tillman announced, sending another wave of excitement through the crowd. 'There are ten things on the grounds of Stonedown you must find and visit. The footman is handing out the papers with the clues and each numbered clue has a corresponding number on the item it describes. Work out the clues and go to the objects to see if you are correct, then you will return here, write out your answers and give them to us. The pair with the most correct answers will receive a fine bottle of brandy to share between them.'

Lord Tillman held up the brandy which made the bored husbands sit up and take notice. 'You will have two hours to find all the objects. In the event of a tie, we will ask questions about the object you saw so pay attention to what you are seeing. A shot will sound when you have fifteen minutes left and then another will tell you when it is time to return. Good luck, everyone, and happy hunting.'

Couples who already had their clues set off in search of their described objects. While Clara and Hugh waited for their copy of the clues, Clara tried to appear pleased and relaxed, but inside she silently sighed. At least the first activity wasn't a sleigh ride, the lack of snow having put paid to any chance of that. Snow or no snow didn't change the fact that she must spend the following two hours combing the Stonedown grounds for landmarks with Hugh. At last, the footman handed her a copy of the clues and Clara pretended to concentrate on them so she wouldn't have to look at Hugh. Lady Fulton strolled by with a swagger that made Clara look up from the parchment.

'It will be an interesting game, won't it, Lady Kingston?' she said, as if this were ample revenge for their exchange of words last night.

'They always are,' Clara responded as calmly as she could, as though this were just another event here and not the second most shocking and uncomfortable experience of her life.

'Well, perhaps you can share in our brandy after we win it, because we will win, won't we, Lord Westbook?'

'We have as good a chance as anyone.' He held out his arm to her and she took it before both of them stepped out into the frosty countryside air.

After that challenge, Clara could no longer stare at the parchment or ignore Hugh. She rose, trying to be polite and gracious even while she wanted to ball up the clues and lob them at the back of Lady Fulton's elegant hat. 'Shall we?'

'Lead the way.' He waved his arm towards the French door left ajar by the last couple who'd passed through it in search of brandy and glory.

Securing the buttons on her gloves against the cold air outside, she stepped on to the stone portico following the line of the house. Just beyond it was the brown lawn leading out towards a copse of trees. The grass, brittle with frost and cold, crunched beneath their boots while they walked, the harsh noise seeming to echo the chill between them.

The heavy silence that had enveloped them at dinner hung over them again like the clouds did the countryside, the weight of it just as oppressive. All around them, Clara could hear the excited chatter and laughter of the other guests enjoying themselves as they struck out in search of their treasures. She glanced at him as they walked side by side in no particular direction, having discussed none of the clues or where they would begin. His face was passive with no hint of disappointment at this unfortunate circumstance, except Clara was tired of disappointment and worry and the constant tension. She didn't wish to spend another Christmas in this state and Hugh Delamare be damned. She would not allow this awkwardness to dominate the week or ruin yet another merry season. He was the past, a very brief moment of it, and she would no longer permit it to command the present.

'I assume you know where we are going?' Hugh asked.

'Just there.' She pointed to the line of trees at the edge of the lawn, eager to be out of sight of the house and far enough away from the other guests to give Hugh a clue of a very different kind. She led him into the shadow of the trees where the temperature noticeably dropped, adding a deeper chill to the already biting air. She was glad for it because it stiffened her resolve even while she clutched her arms around her to stave off the cold. 'We must speak before we can discuss the clues.'

'About what?' Hugh asked, the cold appearing not to trouble him.

She rubbed her arms, fighting off the desire to take the easy path and let him be the one to speak first or to keep pretending that all was well, even when it wasn't. She would not sacrifice a chance at a pleasant Christmas merely to protect her ego from the possibility that she was about to make a bigger fool of herself now than she had with him six years ago, but the matter had to be settled.

'It seems there is some tension between us, if dinner last night is any indication,' she announced with all the directness of her and Adam's old tutor. 'We needn't rehash why this may be, but I hate to ignore it either. What happened between us the last time we were here together was regrettable, but that was a long time ago and a great deal has happened to us both since. I would hate for either of us to have the rest of the week ruined because of it. I'm not asking that we be friends, but that we put the past behind us and be to each other as we would if we'd been paired with anyone else. There's no reason to feel awkward together or ruin a good house party. I hope you agree.'

Clara set her shoulders, waiting to see what reaction this would provoke. She was amazed to see admiration slowly replace his shock.

Hugh stared down at Clara, who spoke to him with the same directness his man of affairs employed whenever he had to deliver bad news about the estate. He admired her ability to be so straightforward. It was a trait he rarely witnessed in any woman, especially not in his last mistress, Lady Frances. Even at the end of the relationship when they'd clearly been together out of habit and not affection, she hadn't possessed the same strength of character as Clara, leaving it to Hugh to end things between them. It had been a relief to both his pocket and his conscience. Other high-born men might dally with one young lady after another and think nothing of the consequences, but having a mistress was something he'd never been comfortable with. A good amount of late nights and cheap brandy had helped to quell his conscience, but it hadn't silenced it completely.

He was glad to see Clara possessed more fortitude than to allow this tension to linger between them and he regretted not being the one to say it first. She was right, their time together six years ago had been brief and although he had cared a great deal for her, far deeper than even he had been able to believe in so short an amount of time, he had made his decision and both of them had gone on to live other lives. Now they were together again and she was calling a halt to the unease that had dominated dinner last night, the one that would continue to annoy them if they didn't face this square on.

'I agree, Lady Kingston. I suspect that we've both come to Stonedown with similar purposes, to enjoy a Christmas of brightness after a few years of dark ones. I don't wish for my presence to prevent you from having what would otherwise be a wonderful holiday. We must put the past behind us and do our best to have fun during the brief time here.' He held out his hand for her to shake.

She stared at it a moment, clearly as aghast by his frankness as he'd been by hers. Hugh's fingers twitched while he waited for her to take his hand and he wondered if she would. Despite the moment at the base of the stairs last night when he'd comforted her, she hadn't been open or kind to him since their reunion. Even her proposal had been all business. There was nothing to say that this agreement between them would do anything more than thaw a touch of the ice surrounding them and things wouldn't continue on as they had since last night, except with a little more conversation.

He was about to pull back his hand and admit the futility of trying to reach out to her when she slowly stretched out her hand and finally took his.

The coldness of the trees overhead seemed to vanish as he stared into her eyes, the clouds of their breath meeting in the space between them. This gesture should have been nothing more than the sealing of a bargain, but it wasn't. While he held on to her, the time that had passed and all the heartache that had filled it between today and six years ago disappeared. She was simply young Clara again and he was taking the first tentative steps towards making her so much more. If he could draw her to him and slide his arm around her waist and bend her into the curve of his body to taste her full lips, he would. He wanted to make her wide eyes close with a sigh while he clasped her small body against his. If he could touch her so intimately, then maybe he could touch the Hugh he used to be, the one not corrupted by disappointment and his own failings, but a man she'd at one time admired and craved.

Instead, he let go of her and lowered his hand, the delicate imprint of her fingers on the back of his as vivid as her pale skin against the darker tones of her hair. They would never again mean what they had to each other back then, but at least the painful stiffness between them and her low opinion of him might change. If he could redeem himself in her eyes and receive her forgiveness, he could redeem himself in everyone's eyes and perhaps forgive himself. It was a goal he longed to obtain.

Clara let go of Hugh, but she didn't step away from him. Instead, she continued to stare at him, doing all she could to hide how stunned she was by his ready agreement and how easily she might have fallen into his arms and repeated all her prior mistakes when his hand had touched hers. When she'd spoken, she'd braced herself, expecting him to laugh off or dismiss her concerns as nothing more than an overactive imagination such as the one she'd employed when she'd thought that he would propose. She hadn't expected this ready agreement or the heat in his eyes that had threatened to melt the icicles hanging on the branches above them. If she had stepped closer to him, tilted back her head in invitation, she was certain he would have taken her in his arms and kissed her, and she wouldn't have stopped him. It was madness and she smoothed her hand over the front of her pelisse, trying to shake the feel of his fingers wrapped around hers, relieved the moment had passed.

I've spent too much time listening to Lady Pariston and Anne and it has muddled my thoughts.

Their tenuous truce would never hold if she fawned on him as she had six years ago. Besides, it was plain that their time together, for whatever it was worth, was long gone and while she might be lonely since Alfred's passing, she wasn't so lonely as to mistake Hugh for a man capable of easing it with both discretion and genuine affection. With a shaking hand she raised the crumpled parchment to read it, thinking they'd better get on with the hunt and stop dallying around before they found themselves in who knew what trouble. 'We should read the clues and see where to go before we run out of time and have no objects to our credit.'

'We can't have that.'

'Imagine how thrilled Lord Westbook and Lady Fulton would be to brag about besting a marquess and a marchioness in something as simple as a game.' She was certain that after the way Lady Fulton had approached her last night and at the start of the game, the woman would continue to do all she could to try to knock Clara down a peg or two. This odd pairing gave her more ammunition to do it with.

'Judging by the way she spoke to you at the start of the hunt, I see you've suffered the privilege of being the topic of one of Lord

Westbook's stories or on the receiving end of Lady Fulton's sharp tongue.'

'More than once. I understand Lord Westbook, but I can't see why Lady Fulton has to be so difficult.'

'Because she's jealous of you.'

'Jealous?' It didn't seem possible.

'By belittling you, she hopes to raise herself up. You have a kindness and beauty that she lacks and where she bargained her money for a title, you achieved yours through love.'

'I'd never considered it that way.' Strange it should be Hugh who pointed it out and called her beautiful. She clasped the sides of the parchment tight against the compliment, afraid to read too much into it. It was his way of honouring the truce and nothing more. 'We can't let them beat us.'

'Then read the clue and let's win this game.'

She cleared her throat and read out the first clue. 'A thing with no hands that helps a man.'

He came to stand behind her, looking over her shoulder at Lady Tillman's fine Italian script. The strong scent of his sandalwood shaving soap made more potent by the crisp morning air took her by surprise. She shook off the temptation to tilt her head back against his shoulder and inhale by reading the words again. She could forgive him for what had happened but it didn't mean she should forget it or what he'd made of himself since. His prior behaviour told her more about him than any of his compliments ever could and she must believe this above all other things. 'What do you think the clue means?'

'Hmmm, something helpful, but with no hands.' Thankfully, he stepped away from her to ponder it, stroking the fine line of his jaw with his fingers, his eyes raised to the sky as if the answer were written in the grey and white clouds passing overhead. In this stance, he reminded her of the boy who used to come to Winsome Manor to study with Adam during holidays, not the wastrel Marquess he'd become. If only he could have held on to that innocence and sense of youth, but, as Clara well knew, mourning had a way of ageing a person. 'A tool, perhaps, something in the carpenter's shed?'

Clara shook her head. 'Lady Tillman may not stand on convention, but she wouldn't send her guests there. No, it has to be something closer to the house.'

Across the lawn and somewhere beyond the trees, they heard other guests talking and laughing while they puzzled out different clues or moved on to a new one.

'We'd better figure it out soon or we'll be the only ones who don't find anything.'

Clara snapped her fingers, her gloves muffling the sound. 'I know what it is. It's a sundial.'

'A clock with no hands and a clock is helpful to man,' Hugh mused. 'Well done, Clara, but where's a sundial? I didn't notice one in the garden when I was out there walking yesterday.'

She ignored his use of her familiar name, guiltily enjoying how it sounded in the deep tones of his voice. She shouldn't allow him to be so familiar with her, but if she chided him for it then the truce might end and the awkwardness she dreaded would return. 'It isn't in the garden, but at the top of a rise in a clearing overlooking the lake.'

'Then lead the way.'

Chapter Four

Clara and Hugh raced along the crushed gravel path that meandered through the trees to where it opened on to the lake near the bottom of a gently sloping hill. Along the bank of the lake, the path continued, disappearing up into a thick patch of trees that sat on a small hill overlooking the water.

'There's the path,' Clara announced when they were out in the open. Taking up the hem of her skirt, she made for it and Hugh followed close beside her. Their progress slowed a touch when the ground began to rise, the pace of their breathing increasing as each step became a little harder.

'Are you sure there's anything up there?' Hugh asked, not nearly as winded as Clara during the climb. Through the thick branches, they could barely see the lake or believe that this tangle of leafless ash and oak trees would ever break into something open.

'Yes, I'm certain it's there, but the area around the path has grown up so much I think most people who were aware of it have forgotten the way. The rest probably don't know it's here.'

'What makes you remember it so well?'

She raised her hem a little higher to step over a fallen branch. 'My mother and I used to walk here during our visits with Father for the hunting season. The view of Stonedown from the top is magnificent.' The closer they drew to the crest the quicker Clara moved despite the exertion of the climb and the constant dodging of rocks and dead branches. For a moment this was more than a scavenger hunt, but a brief chance to touch a part of her past that was as painful as the loss of her husband. With the stone sundial coming into view, the memory of her and her mother racing out from the line of the trees to see who could reach it first overcame her. She'd always win and her mother would laugh before standing with her arm around Clara to take in the view of Stonedown. Clara didn't race to the sundial this morning, but approached it with solemn reverence, the happy memory bittersweet. She was tired of mourning, of losing and regretting, and yet here she stood at this once-meaningful site with Hugh, one of the most potent regrets she'd ever endured.

She touched the sundial, running her hand along the front of it. So many times she'd tried to puzzle out the time, but reading the sundial, unlike retaining some Latin, was a skill she'd never mastered no matter how many times her mother had demonstrated how to do it. With no sun out today, there wasn't even the chance to try. She missed her mother and father and the happy days as a family with them at Winsome before their passing had left her with an inheritance and all the insecurities of a young woman without a mother to guide her through the pitfalls of society. If her mother had lived, perhaps Clara wouldn't have stumbled with Hugh, or been left to find her own way when it came to dresses and carrying herself and dealing with people like Lady Fulton.

Clara's melancholy turn must have shown on her face for Hugh came up on the opposite side of the sundial and rested his big hands on the solid surface.

'Are you all right?' he asked.

Clara thought of some flippant answer she could give him about being winded from their walk, but, like the real concern he'd shown her on the stairs last night, it was clear by the grave tone of his voice that he genuinely wanted to know. She owed his kindness a touch of truth untainted by any past bitterness. 'I was thinking of my mother and how much I miss her and my father at this time of year. Some days it feels as if I've spent too many Christmases mourning loved ones.'

'I know.' He tapped one carved Roman numeral with his fingers. 'Three Christmases before we…' The rest of the sentence drifted away with the breeze. Clara nodded to tell him he didn't need to speak the words because, like him, she knew the story, too. He said nothing more about the incident as he continued. 'I lost my father. It was difficult that first season to look around the table and realise someone so important was missing and how much that loss had changed me and everything. Then, after Hermione and my mother, every year has grown harder to bear. It's a lonely table now.'

'I know. Loss changes so much,' Clara whispered, once again struck by how strange it was that she could talk with him about her grief without shame or embarrassment. She shouldn't do so, but after keeping it bottled up for so long, afraid people would tire of listening to it or tell her that she should move past it, it was nice to speak with someone who genuinely understood, even if that someone was Hugh.

Hugh peered out over the water, the rippled surface of which had turned silver with the grey clouds covering the sky above it. Loss had changed him a great deal, far more than he cared to dwell on either silently or with Clara. He'd gone from the son of a marquess who'd been willing to set aside the desires of his own heart to do his duty to his family to a wastrel in London, cursing duty and determined to blot out the pain and guilt of his wife's loss through wine and women. He'd done everything asked of him and it still hadn't mattered and yet, in turning his back on his responsibilities, he'd made the pain even worse.

'You miss your wife?' Clara's sweet voice drew him away from the torment of his mistakes and back to her and the stunning countryside surrounding them.

'You seem surprised,' Hugh countered, but not in accusation. Hers had been a soft question of surprise and Hugh wasn't upset by Clara asking it. Everyone had known that his and Hermione's marriage had not been a love match.

'The last three years might indicate otherwise.'

'My exploits in London were greatly exaggerated.'

'All the actresses, you mean?'

'Yes. There were one or two, but their company is not as enjoyable as that of a woman of quality.' Hugh swallowed hard, sick again at the kind of man he'd become. He only hoped it wasn't too late to redeem himself and become again the honourable and noble man he'd once been.

'But still you dallied.'

'There are many reasons a man seeks out diversions in London, sometimes it's to be reckless and sometimes it's to forget. Hermione and I may not have gone to the altar in love, but we came to love one another through our work to finish what my father and mother had started at Everburgh. She shared my desire and willingness to do whatever it took to rebuild it and to make sacrifices to see that it, and the line, endured.'

He balled his fists against the pain, not sure why he was telling Clara this. They were not intimates or confidants, but in the soft, patient manner with which she regarded him, he couldn't hold back. In London, there had been many people willing to drink and carouse with him, but none eager to listen to or ease the grief he carried, the one he'd tried to ignore and forget with one more glass of brandy or one more evening with Lady Frances. When he'd run into Adam in London last Season, he'd thought his old friend someone he could confide in, but Adam and Anne were too happily married and certain of the solidness of their life together for Adam to do more than listen with sympathy. He couldn't understand Hugh's pain the way Clara did. 'The day I lost Hermione was one of the most difficult of my life. She'd been with child, but lost it early. All should have been well and we should have gone on to have more chances and time together but the midwife, and later the doctor, couldn't stop the bleeding. When I pressed them for answers, all they could say was that sometimes this happens and they didn't know why. That night, I sat with her, encouraging and willing her to live, but the weaker she grew, the less she heard me until she was gone. I should have known she wasn't meant to have children and been more cautious with her, but she wanted so much to do her duty as a marchioness and give me a son that she hid the true depth of her weakness from me and everyone.'

'You aren't to blame for what happened.' Clara reached out and covered his hand with hers, the motion impulsive and uncalculated, just as she'd always been. 'Sadly, it's all too common even with the strongest of women.'

'But she died for nothing. I married her for money. I admit that, but I didn't do it out of greed. I did it to preserve everything my parents spent their lives trying to achieve. Although I came to love her, even her dowry wasn't enough to make Everburgh completely safe or free from worry. Despite every sacrifice that I and Hermione made, I'm still dealing with problems and on the verge of losing everything again. It's the reason I turned my back on duty when I was in London, for I did my duty and Hermione tried to do hers, and what did it gain us? Nothing.' Hugh wanted to smash the sundial to pieces until the pain inside him was smashed, too. Duty had once been the noblest reason for anyone to act, but it had become a chain that could kill the people bound to him, including his parents and his wife. He took a deep breath and unclenched his hand, refusing to allow the dark hate and anger that had nearly trampled him in London to claim him once again. 'Without her I was lost and a lost man is apt to lose his way in other regards.'

'I'm sure you'll soon find your way again.' Clara's grip on his hand tightened and she leaned towards him with a conviction to admire. 'I'm trying to find my way, too.'

'You don't seem as if you've lost your head.' He turned his hand over in hers and held it tight. Their gloves separated their flesh, but not the warmth between them and he clung to it and her, drawing comfort from both.

'I have in my own way. After Alfred's

death, I cloistered myself at Winsome, avoiding the world and thinking that in doing so I could stop the pain, but it only made it worse. I can't live like that, without hope or prospect of a better future, nor would Alfred have wanted me to.'

'You don't deserve to be unhappy, but to enjoy life here or wherever you choose.'

'Some day we'll both be happy and all this awful business will be behind us, not entirely forgotten, but not so present and troubling.' She smiled and the sight of it swept the chill off Hugh in a way nothing else in the last three years, not all the brandy or his time with his mistress or anything, ever had.

'Yes, we will.' He gently squeezed her hand, eager to hold on to her and the contentment surrounding them for as long as he could, but it didn't last. From somewhere in the trees behind them, the voices of a man and woman made the birds stop twittering and Clara let go of Hugh.

'This way, I tell you it's here. I used to come here with my mother,' Adam's voice declared as he tugged Anne out of the line of the trees and into the clearing. They held hands, laughing and smiling, the love and ease between them obvious and admirable. There were few among their class who could claim such joy in their union, but Anne and Adam's marriage had been a love match, one for any couple to admire and emulate. Hugh hoped very much that he and Clara might soon meet people who would allow them to join their ranks. The fleeting thought that they could find such happiness together whispered through his mind before he pushed it aside.

Adam and Anne jerked to a halt, but the laughing smiles on their faces only grew wider. They exchanged a knowing look and Hugh could practically feel the heat of Clara's blush from across the sundial. Thankfully they hadn't caught Hugh and Clara holding hands. Their gesture of comfort was innocent enough, but Hugh knew other people wouldn't take it that way. Thankfully, it was Anne and Adam who'd stumbled on them. They would be more discreet than someone like Lord Westbook, but how the two of them felt about what some might view as Hugh dallying with Clara again remained to be seen. Blaming it on the spirit of the game would only go so far and like society and Sir Nathaniel's good opinion, Adam's was one that Hugh didn't wish to lose.

'I see you figured this out, too, Clara,' Adam called to his sister, striding forward, his wife's hand in his, the bliss between them and their freedom to revel in it enviable.

'It wasn't too difficult. How many other clues have you worked out?' Clara recovered herself with admiration, but there was no missing that the red colour of her cheeks was from more than the cold.

'Five, we're halfway done. How about you two? What have you worked out so far?'

'Just the one.' Clara limply motioned to the sundial and the number one affixed to it.

'Then we'd better stop dawdling over the view and get on with it, shouldn't we, Lady Kingston?' Hugh suggested. He wasn't about to give Adam and Anne any more to talk about by acting like a schoolboy caught skipping lessons.

This snapped Clara out of her shock and the blush disappeared from her cheeks as she faced her brother and sister-in-law. 'Yes, we must, because we're determined to win, aren't we, Lord Delamare?'

'Indeed we are.' He threw Anne and Adam

a wave, ignoring the shock that decorated their faces at this change in Clara's attitude towards Hugh as he and Clara set off for the path. 'Good luck to you both.'

'And good luck to you,' Anne sang after them, but Hugh ushered Clara away before she could singe her delicate cheeks with any more blushes.

Clara hurried down the hill faster than she'd raced up it, needing the quick activity to shake off the unease of Anne and Adam having almost happened upon them in the clearing and the confusion created by her conversation with Hugh. If her brother and sister-in-law had stepped out of the trees sooner or without warning, they would've caught Clara and Hugh in a most compromising position, one Clara still couldn't believe she'd stumbled into. She hadn't intended to touch Hugh out of comfort or any other emotion, but she'd been unable to help herself. No one deserved to suffer the loss of their cherished spouse. For all the wrong Hugh had done her, she wouldn't wish that sorrow on her worst enemy and she couldn't ignore it when it was in front of her either. His pain was so similar to what she'd endured these last two years and she'd wanted to drive it away as Anne and Adam had done so many times for her. It had also surprised her.

Despite the dubious beginning of his union with Lady Hermione, whose family's shipping wealth had given them more money than hers could ever have hoped to possess, Clara was glad the woman had garnered his love. During the Seasons that Clara had been in London with Alfred, she'd seen more than one arranged marriage falter from the start, leaving each person wishing for the passing of the other in order to free them. That Hugh and Lady Hermione had come to love one another, and that his reasons for marrying her had been guided by duty to his family and not simply greed, altered so much of what she'd come to believe about Hugh. For so long, she'd been unable to see anything except the calculating bargain that Hugh had struck at her expense but, as Adam had once tried to tell her, there had been a great deal more to his decision.

However, for all the comfort they'd offered one another and the relief and calm it had given them, and for all the ways his words had begun to change her opinion of him, a small warning continued to play in the back of her mind. It'd sounded when they'd touched across the stone and it continued to assert itself while she walked beside him. She should be more cautious with her feelings and his and better mind her emotions in his presence, but in the face of his tender questions she'd been helpless to resist being open with him. She hoped he didn't make her regret it as he had before for there were a number of days left in the house party and, as she'd learned with him last time, his preference for her could change at a moment's whim. He might have had honourable reasons for leaving her, but in the end he had still chosen someone else over her and she must remember this and the kind of man he'd become since. His motives for doing what he'd done in London didn't excuse it and the fact that a man with his privileges who could have chosen any distraction had selected the basest ones seemed to say more about him than what he'd told her. She would do well to heed the warning and to not allow her opinion of him to soften so much that she forgot herself again with him. They could be friendly with one another, but not friends and certainly not, as Lady Pariston had suggested last night, more.

At last, Hugh and Clara reached the beginning of the path that led back to the house and the rest of the clues and stopped to catch their breath.

'Where do we go next?' Hugh asked, his voice steady as if nothing on the rise had happened, or it hadn't meant as much or been as confusing to him as it had been to Clara. This was probably closer to the truth than anything else Clara wished to believe.

Clara read the second clue, determined to be as aloof and unruffled by what had happened as Hugh. 'Holiday sweets are made sweeter and brighter by me, the fruit of this tree, round like a globe and disliking the cold.'

'Nothing but apples and plums grow in this part of England and they can tolerate the cold,' Hugh mused, remaining a polite distance away from Clara, seemingly aware of how close they'd come to trouble at the sundial and unwilling to have it happen again. With them at the bottom of the rise near the lake, anyone in search of the first object could happen upon them. After having inadvertently thrown caution to the wind at the sundial, Clara appreciated his caution here, even if all this restraint and the constant shifting of emotions where Hugh was concerned was beginning to wear on her. Being so serious was not what she'd come to Stonedown to do. She did enough of that at home.

Clara read the clue twice more. On the third reading, the answer came to her. 'Oranges. The clue is oranges.'

Hugh looked sceptical. 'They don't grow here in the winter.'

'They do in the orangery near the stables. Lord Tillman has a fine specimen and it's always laden with fruit at this time of year. As children, Adam and I loved the treat.' She couldn't wait to see it again.

'Then that must be it.'

'There's only one way to know.'

'I'll race you to it,' Hugh challenged with a rogue's wink that Clara couldn't help but answer. Despite the cold it was a beautiful day and the sun cutting through the clouds and the naked branches of the trees couldn't help but infect her soul. It was difficult to remain morose or introspective in the middle of such gorgeous countryside, especially with Hugh teasing her into a race. It'd been a long time since she'd run like a girl in short dresses and she missed the freedom of it.

'Ready. Set. Go.' She took off before she was even done speaking, darting out ahead of Hugh like she used to do with Adam whenever they would race as children.

Behind her she could hear the fast fall of Hugh's feet when he set off after her, his long stride allowing him to quickly pass her before they even reached the turn in the trees where they'd called their truce. He glanced over his shoulder and, seeing her far behind, slowed down until she caught up to him.

She raced past him, forcing him to catch up, but this time he didn't pass her, but kept pace, the two of them flying down the path, his delight in running matching hers.

Then the glass roof of the orangery and the weathervane on the stables came into view over the tops of the trees. The closer they drew the stronger the earthy scent of horses grew and Clara's excitement increased. The crush of the gravel beneath her feet and the sharp breeze stinging her cheeks was the way it used to be when she and Adam had run along these paths with her parents. The joy of those carefree days filled her, lightening her steps and her heart. It amazed her that such a marvellous time should be had with Hugh, but it didn't matter, nor did the past or the future or her opinions, nothing except this did. It was exactly what she'd come to Stonedown to find.

They continued their quick pace until they turned the bend in the path and almost collided with Sir Nathaniel and Mrs Alton. Jerking to a halt, they couldn't help but laugh through their winded apologies for the near miss.

'I see you two are getting on well,' Sir Nathaniel observed with a smile as wide as Hugh's. His round nose was so red from the cold it was almost the same shade as his maroon redingote. 'With all this hurrying you must have solved many clues.'

'Not at all. We're racing to catch up.' Clara laughed through her hard breath, her joy spreading to Mrs Alton who flashed Clara and Hugh a friendly smile.

'Then I wish you great success.' Sir Nathaniel turned to Hugh. 'Before you go, Lord Delamare, I want you to know I sent a letter to the solicitor I recommended this morning. You should hear from him shortly. I told him that I know you and instructed him to give your matter his full attention. I don't do that for everyone, only those I like.'

'Thank you, Sir Nathaniel.' Hugh sobered, taking the man's hand and giving it a firm shake. 'Your support and regard mean a great deal to me.'

'Now off you go so Mrs Alton and I may venture on to our next destination.' With a raise of his beaver hat, Sir Nathaniel bid them goodbye and escorted the quiet Mrs Alton away.

'Come on, we're losing time.' Hugh took hold of Clara's hand and pulled her along the path.

Everything inside Clara told her to let go of him, but she held on tight, too afraid to open her fingers and be sent whirling from the many shocks of today, including the one Sir Nathaniel had lobbed at her. She'd known the man for years. He was well regarded by many, but it often took a great deal for him to regard others well. That he'd looked on Hugh with respect and offered to help him was amazing. At the sundial, she'd assured

Hugh that he would find his way back to a more respectful life and it was clear from Sir Nathaniel's regard that he was already on that road. It called into question once again all Clara's opinions of him, ones she didn't wish to think of right now for fear they would mar her enjoyment of the day.

They approached the glass dome of the orangery and the riot of greenery and flowers inside. The vivid colours were a sharp contrast to the grey and brown landscape outside the glass and iron door. Hugh let go of her and pulled it open. Clara flexed her fingers as she stepped inside, the heat and warmth hitting her as hard as the loss of Hugh's grasp. They shouldn't have held hands, especially when they'd passed the stables and the stable hands inside attending to the horses that stood snorting and neighing in their stalls. She remembered how fast the maids had informed Lord Westbook of Hugh's engagement last time. They didn't need the grooms whispering anything to their aristocratic riders, but the gesture had been so much in the spirit of the game that she didn't mind. It was the loss of their joy she would mind more if she chided him for being so familiar so she said nothing.

'This wasn't here when I last visited.' Hugh studied the ornate and sweet-smelling flowers lined up in pots on trestle tables along the glass walls.

'It was, but a hail storm had damaged it that autumn. Lord Tillman worked hard to save the tree, but he lost almost everything else,' Clara explained as they moved towards the orange tree in the centre. It rose out of a large hole in the stone floor, the slick green leaves dotted here and there with sumptuous round oranges. 'He's spent the last six years reviving it. Isn't it amazing?'

'It is.'

Hugh felt a little like the greenery around him and the tree, as though he'd been torn down and ruined and was fighting to rebuild. He'd gained Sir Nathaniel's regard and hopefully with it an advantage with his case and he was, in this small way, proving to Clara that he wasn't the cad she believed him to be. He, like the tree with the oranges he reached up to touch, wasn't beyond saving and apparently others beside Adam were capable of seeing it.

'There's the number two.' Hugh pointed to the paper number tied with a ribbon around the tree's trunk. 'What's our next clue?'

'I almost hate to leave here.' Clara sighed. 'It's so cold outside.'

'We'll lose if we stay and then we'll have to endure all Lady Fulton's bragging if she and Lord Westbook win.'

'I suppose you're right.' Clara didn't look at the parchment, but continued to take in the tree, tilting her head in thought to one side and making the curls at the back of her head brush her pink cheeks. She found contentment beneath the tree, one he hadn't witnessed either on the stairs, at dinner, or even at the sundial. He'd only seen it grace her face once before, six years ago when they'd stood beneath another bit of greenery, the flush of their first kiss making her cheeks as ruddy as they were today. He tapped his fingers together, almost able to feel the mistletoe berry he'd plucked from the branch, Clara still in his arms, the taste of her lingering on his lips.

Hugh opened the top button of his black

redingote to give him some ease from the heat of the orangery and continued to watch her, captivated by the delicate line of her jaw above the raised collar of her pelisse and the flush of heat that gave colour to her skin. When he'd glanced over his shoulder to see her running so far behind him, smiling like she used to do when they'd ridden together in the sleigh six years ago, he'd wanted to turn and take her in his arms, to sweep her off her feet and spin her in a circle until her laughter silenced all the birds in the forest.

He and their time together had brought that smile to her face and he didn't want to lose it. Not even when they'd come upon Sir Nathaniel had her exuberance dimmed. She hadn't looked on Hugh like some pariah, but had smiled and laughed with an infectious ease that had cast a spell over him until he'd been able to forget himself and everything and just be with her. Even now he should be urging them to continue with the scavenger hunt so he could return to the men and Sir Nathaniel and work to secure their help in ending the threat to Everburgh, but he couldn't tear himself away from Clara and this moment. It would mean losing the ability to regard her unobserved and force him to act as if each time their hands touched or her voice rang out in the clear crisp air that she didn't enchant him.

He turned away from her to view the tree, resisting this captivation and the desire to be anything more than friendly with her. He'd had good reasons for giving her up six years ago, a commitment to honour and duty that had cost Hermione her life and Hugh a piece of his soul. But he could no more go back and change what had happened between him and Clara than he could bring back Hermione and, until he was certain again of the solidness of those old beliefs and what they meant to him and his life, he could be certain of little else. Besides, after her greeting in the library yesterday, anything more than friendship would be viewed with nothing but distrust, especially with Everburgh still in needs of funds to battle the pending court challenge.

With a great deal of reluctance, he did up the top button of his coat, determined to focus on the hunt. He was required to be her partner, not to pester her by wailing about his miseries or what had happened before.

They would have fun and they would win and that's all they'd have between them. 'What's the next clue?'

The following two hours were a joy for Clara as she and Hugh hurried from one part of Stonedown to another. The clues led them inside the large house and then back out to the garden and many other places of note. They passed numerous other guests during their travels and each couple smiled and waved to the other while teasing them that they were going to win the brandy. The good-natured teasing didn't hide the surprise that decorated many faces at the sight of Clara and Hugh so easy in one another's company, especially after their noticeable silence at dinner last night. Clara could almost hear people whispering in amazement about it as they left them, but she didn't care. Let them say what they liked about her and Hugh. She was enjoying herself in a way she hadn't done in a very long time and she wouldn't allow anyone or anything to ruin it.

At last, with the pale sunlight hidden behind the clouds beginning to dim enough to tell them that their time for the search was drawing to a close and that the early evening darkness of winter would soon force all but the stoutest of souls back inside, she and Hugh studied the last clue.

'Pages of sparkling gold and red easy to ignore in its progress through the year but standing ever ready for those who care to notice,' Clara read again.

Hugh slipped the parchment out from between her gloved fingertips and read it again. 'What do you think it is?'

'I can't say. The other clues seemed so obvious once we really thought about them, but not this one.'

'You're to thank for that. Without your knowledge of Stonedown, we never would have deciphered most of the clues.'

'But you guessed the peacock bench in the garden.'

He glanced up at her from across the paper. 'Only because that wasn't one of Lady Tillman's more difficult clues, but this is.'

He furrowed his brow as he considered the last clue, concentrating on it as if it were a faro table and he was waiting for his ball to land on his number, except of all the stories she'd heard of him in London, gambling had never been one of them. He hadn't been known for his outrageous bets or nights spent at the tables losing far more than he could afford. His stories had involved fast carriage rides down Rotten Row with questionable company beside him during the fashionable hour and at least one duel that he'd won without doing more damage to his opponent than sending a ball through his fine wool coat. Some said he'd deliberately aimed wide to spare his opponent and that if he hadn't his lethal aim would have split the man's skull. Clara shivered from more than the cold, finding it hard to reconcile the London Hugh with the one before her who'd shown so much delight in this simple game and so much tenderness with her at the sundial. Part of her wanted to ask him about the incident, but she held her tongue, unwilling to end the good will between them with questions about his curious past.

In the distance, from the direction of the house, the warning shot sounded.

'We only have fifteen more minutes.'

I should have been concentrating on the clue and not Hugh.

She hated to think that their missing this

last item might mean the difference between them and Lord Westbook and Lady Fulton winning. She wasn't sure how they'd done in the game for they'd only passed them once, but they'd both seemed very sure of their progress.

'Then we must think and fast.'

Clara peered over his forearm at the wrinkled and torn paper, for he was too tall for her to look over his shoulder. It brought her cheek close to his arm and, if this had been six years ago, she could have laid her head on his chest and let him wrap his arm around her shoulder while they struggled to figure out Lady Tillman's clue. But this wasn't six years ago and, for all the holding of hands on the way to the orangery, they hadn't touched since. She had no desire to make this awkward by reaching out to him again.

'I know what it is.' Hugh jerked up straight, his face brightening with realisation that made Clara bounce a little on her toes. 'It's the illuminated manuscript.'

'Of course,' Clara exclaimed. 'The ink is red and gold and it follows the liturgical year.'

'Let's go and make certain.'

She followed him around the side of the

house and up the back stairs of the portico, certain that when they reached the library the number ten hanging on the bookstand would confirm that he was right. Victory was only one room in Stonedown away and she couldn't wait to seize it. From across the different areas of the estate she could see people trickling in together to form small groups and discuss the hunt. Hugh pulled open the French doors leading into a small sitting room off the back of the house. They both sighed with relief and delight at the heat that greeted them and began to remove their gloves and open the buttons of their thick coats as they crossed the room and stepped into the hall leading to the library.

There, on one of the benches lining the long wall, sat Lady Pariston and Lord Wortley. It was an odd but charming pairing that one who didn't know better might mistake for a grandmother and her grandson, but there was no mistaking the defeat making their shoulders slump.

'Lady Pariston, Lord Wortley, how did you fair?' Clara hated to see them looking so dejected.

'Not well I'm afraid, Lady Kingston.' Lord

Wortley stood and bowed, his manners perfect, but his voice, like his frame, not having reached its full potential. 'Lady Pariston was unable to walk the grounds.'

'My hips hate the cold,' Lady Pariston explained with more unhappy regret than elderly complaint.

'We've been trying to work out the clues without actually visiting them but I'm afraid we haven't fared well for I don't know the estate, but I believe Lady Pariston did an excellent job guessing many of the items, even if we couldn't prove it.' To his credit, the young man demonstrated no bitterness about being held back from activities by his aged partner who appeared more sorry than he did at having been unable to fully partake in the festivities.

'I told the young man to go ahead without me and have fun, but he wouldn't leave me. I think it was very kind of him to sit here and keep an old lady company.' She patted him tenderly on the arm. 'Even if it means we don't have a shot at winning that brandy and I so love a small taste of it now and again. It helps with my rheumatism.'

'What answers do you have?' Hugh motioned to see their paper. Being in the house, they'd been able to write down their answers.

Lord Wortley gave it to Hugh and he and Clara studied it.

'You have done remarkably well,' Hugh complimented.

They were only missing the last two.

'I'm sure if I'd had more time, I could have come to the correct answers.' Lady Pariston sighed. 'But my memory, like my hips, isn't what it used to be.'

Instead of giving the paper back to them, Hugh slipped their answers behind his, then offered Lady Pariston his arm. 'May I escort you into the sitting room?'

His offer brought the smile back to her aged face. 'Yes, I would like that very much.'

He and Lord Wortley helped her to her feet. With one hand grasping her walking stick tight and the other firmly fixed on Hugh's arm, she allowed him to lead her into the sitting room.

'May I, Lady Kingston?' Lord Wortley offered Clara his slender arm, his chest puffed out in pride at being able to escort her.

'Yes, you may.' She took hold of his arm and they followed Hugh and Lady Pariston down the hall, through the main entrance hall and into the sitting room.

While they walked, Lord Wortley commented on the weather, the food at dinner last night and all the other polite topics required by the conventions of conversation.

Clara didn't hear much of what Lord Wortley said for she was too busy watching Hugh and Lady Pariston. Hugh's tenderness with the Dowager Countess, his easy way with her and his ability to elicit more than one smile or laugh from her touched Clara. Lady Pariston had appeared so downtrodden in the hallway, but now she looked as if this had been her best scavenger hunt ever. Hugh had no reason to be cordial and kind to her but he was, just as he'd been with Clara. It surprised her and left her wondering. Today, he'd acted like the Hugh she'd known as a girl and nothing like the London rake she'd heard so many stories about. Perhaps this was all for show, but his movements and words seemed so natural that it was hard to believe that he was this good a charlatan. Maybe this was the Hugh that Adam and Anne were able to see and Clara should give him the benefit of the doubt as her brother and sister-in-law did. No, it couldn't be or he wouldn't have so many sordid stories attached to his name.

A wave of conversation met them when they entered the front sitting room where the other teams had gathered to exchange stories about the scavenger hunt and how well they had or hadn't done. A group of gentlemen stood around the writing table where a number of quills and inkstands had been set out so the players could write down their answers before handing their papers to Lord Tillman. Hugh escorted Lady Pariston to the comfiest of the two armchairs flanking the fire and helped her to sit.

'If you three wish to stay here and warm yourselves, I will turn in the answers,' Hugh offered and, with a bow, made for the writing desk. He was stopped halfway across the room by Lord Westbook who held up his own sheet, seeming to gloat over his and Lady Fulton's progress. Hugh said nothing in reply, but bent over the table, took up a quill and wrote out their answers. He then handed both pieces of parchment to Lord Tillman. Hugh did not immediately return to Clara, enticed into conversation by Sir Nathaniel instead.

Disappointment dogged Clara at Hugh

remaining across the room, but she tried to shake it off. He'd been in her company for the past two hours. She wasn't surprised he wanted someone new to talk to, especially a man like Sir Nathaniel who was going to help him with his case. Clara knew very little of the legal matter facing Hugh, having avoided bringing it up during their hunt in an effort to not ruin their good time, but she knew it had something to do with Everburgh and its future ownership. She would have to ask Anne about it for she always seemed to hear everything about everyone, especially where Hugh's details were concerned. Unlike Lord Westbook, she was far more discreet with her knowledge.

As if hearing Clara thinking about her, Anne appeared at her elbow. Taking hold of Clara's arm, Anne drew her to the other side of the large marble mantel and away from Lord Wortley and Lady Pariston. Mischief burned in her green eyes as bright as the candles scattered about the room to add additional light on this cloudy day.

'Did you and Lord Delamare enjoy the scavenger hunt?' Anne asked, certain she and

Adam had stumbled upon something more than a deep conversation about mourning.

'Yes, we did.' Clara hoped a direct answer would put an end to this line of questioning. It didn't.

'Did you, now?' Anne prodded.

Clara tilted her head and pinned her with a chastising look. 'Nothing happened between us and nothing is going to happen between us.'

Anne ignored what should have been a silencing glare. 'That's not what it looked like when we saw you.'

'Whatever you have in mind you can go ahead and dismiss it. We are simply enjoying ourselves and that is all.'

'Be sure to enjoy yourself a little bit more while we're here,' Anne suggested 'You never know what might happen.'

Anne made off to join Adam, leaving Clara to shake her head at her sister-in-law's insinuation. It seemed being in the country was more boring for Anne than it was for Clara if she was willing to make up all kinds of fanciful notions about other people, especially Clara. Thankfully, there had been no single male visitors to Winsome of late or who knew what other possible romances Anne might have concocted for Clara.

Once everyone had turned in their answers, Lord and Lady Tillman spent another few moments examining them before Lord Tillman placed one on top of the stack and raised a silencing hand. 'We have our winners.'

The chattering died out as everyone waited to hear who it was. Clara exchanged a triumphant glance with Hugh, certain they would be among those caught in a tie, if not the outright winners. Unfortunately, Lord Westbook and Lady Fulton appeared just as smug from where they sat on an overstuffed ottoman. Clara hoped she and Hugh had bested them. They deserved a little harmless comeuppance for all their arrogant love of gossip and belittling.

'In the past, people have accused me and Lady Tillman of writing clues that were too easy,' Lord Tillman explained, leaving them in suspense a little longer.

A few heads nodded in agreement.

'Judging by the results this year, I think we've greatly improved. In fact, there was only one team that got all the answers correct.'

Speculation swept through the room and Clara exchanged an excited glance with Hugh, knowing they'd found everything. He met her eyes with a humility she couldn't fathom. Whatever the reason for his look, there was no time to consider it as Lord Tillman announced the winners.

'The team with all the correct answers is…' He paused, causing everyone who was sitting to perch on the edge of their seats.

'Get on with it, man,' Mr Alton urged and everyone laughed.

'Lady Pariston and Lord Wortley.'

The surprise on Lord Wortley and Lady Pariston's faces was equal to that of the enthusiastic clapping that greeted the announcement. Lord Wortley looked back and forth from Hugh to Clara, as amazed and perplexed as she was. He opened his mouth to protest the proclamation, but Hugh crossed the room and clapped the young lord vigorously on the back in congratulation.

'You and Lady Pariston deserve this honour more than anyone else.' Hugh's heavy-handed congratulation made Lord Wortley stumble a bit and stopped him from saying whatever he'd intended to say. 'I hope you very much enjoy the proceeds of your winnings.'

Lord Tillman stepped forward with the brandy and presented it to Lady Pariston who smiled as brightly as she had when Hugh had escorted her into the sitting room. No more was said about the paper not being theirs as they held up the bottle in triumph together and received the congratulations of the entire room.

Hugh stepped away from them and came over to join Clara.

'I assume you didn't accidentally mistake the papers when you set our names to them?' Clara asked in a low voice, the rousing chatter in the room covering their conversation.

'No, I didn't. I hope you don't mind, but I thought they deserved a little joy and triumph more than we did.'

'I don't mind at all.' It was worth their losing to see the delight making Lady Pariston beam and Lord Wortley stand a foot taller, and to realise that Hugh had given up their victory for no other reason than kindness. It made her wonder again whether she'd judged Hugh too harshly, for in one afternoon he'd made it very hard for her to hold on to her poor opinion of him and to forget that he was a man not to be trusted. Except she wouldn't trust him, not entirely, until she could figure out who was the real Hugh, the man she'd spent time with today or the London rake.

Chapter Five

Clara stood in front of the full-length mirror in her bedroom, turning from side to side to admire the fourth dress she's tried on in the last fifteen minutes. Last night she'd attempted to not give a great deal of attention to her attire until Anne had commented on it. Tonight, what she wore seemed to take on too much importance. She longed to appear at her best without looking too contrived in her efforts, all the while lamenting the overly simple styles of her dresses.

Only because I wish to show Lady Fulton that I am not a dowdy mouse, she tried to tell herself, but deep down she knew this was a lie. She cared about her attire because she would be beside Hugh again.

She'd greeted him this morning with very

low expectations and he'd defied every one of them, leaving her unsure what to think about him, and all of Anne's teasing didn't help. Under the spell of the scavenger hunt, he'd been the old Hugh she used to admire, but when she was alone with nothing but her past slights and memories it was hard to hold on to this view of him. Hugh could be tricking everyone about his change, using his friendliness and charming personality to draw them in, or it could be real. Unlike the steady grip of his hand against hers today, she couldn't be sure. She twisted the ring on her finger as she took in her reflection, wishing her mother were here. She would be able to ferret out the truth about Hugh, for Clara didn't know what to think, but her mother wasn't here and Clara must decide for herself. If she were thinking clearly, and not battered by old memories of Alfred, her parents and past times at Stonedown, she might be better able to see the truth, but it was so difficult at present.

She dropped her hands to her sides and stood up straight, getting a hold of herself.

There's no need to lose your mind or waffle like a chicken with its head cut off.

There was no reason to rush to form any opinion about Hugh or to be crystal clear about anything except that she must be friendly with him. There was nothing more to it. During her and Hugh's last visit here, the desire to unite their lives had seized them so quickly that she hadn't stopped to think about consequences or difficulties and it had cost her a great deal. It wasn't the case this time. Perhaps, during dinner and the rest of the activities, she might better observe him and uncover more of the man worthy of Adam's friendship, the one she'd caught glimpses of during the scavenger hunt. If so, then she would change her opinion of him. If not, then so be it. There was nothing more to it, certainly not enough for her to fret and worry, except there was.

A small part of her, the one that had taken comfort in his presence last night at the foot of the stairs and again at the sundial, the one that had laughed so easily with him during the hunt, wanted the changes in him to be real. If they were, then maybe the joy she'd experienced with him today could be hers again and she could finally stop worrying about their past and simply enjoy the present.

In the meantime, she must finish dressing for dinner and look the part of the Marchioness of Kingston.

'What do you think, Mary? This one or the dark blue one?' Clara asked the maid who stood patiently nearby, waiting for instructions to either do up the buttons or to choose another dress from the dwindling selection of gowns.

'This one suits you the best, my lady. The gold embroidery on the sleeves makes your necklace sparkle and gives your skin such a nice hue.'

Clara wanted to believe her, but wondered if the maid simply wanted to end this torturous routine and go downstairs to join the servants for supper. Clara would summon Anne for her opinion if she thought it wouldn't garner more teasing about Clara and Hugh. It was another decision she must make on her own.

Taking one last look in the mirror and knowing the dinner gong would soon ring, Clara decided to trust Mary's opinion. 'I believe this dress will do, but I wonder about the others. Lady Exton is right, everything I have is so dark.'

It was difficult to impress people like Lady Fulton when one dressed like a wraith.

'Some of your older dresses are much cheerier in style. Perhaps you would like me to send to Winsome to have a number of them fetched?' Mary suggested.

Such a ridiculous use of time and effort by the servants would normally have made Clara decline, but the more she thought of the pink, yellow and light green dresses she hadn't worn since before Alfred's passing, the ones she'd purchased in London, the more the idea appealed to her. 'It probably wouldn't hurt to have them here. After all, I don't know what other events Lady Tillman has planned and I wouldn't want to appear too dour or wear the same dress twice.'

That was something only a simple country mouse did.

'I'll see to it at once, my lady.' Mary dipped a curtsy that hid her smile, as if she'd known this would be the answer and didn't believe for a second Clara's practical reason for sending for the dresses.

The dinner gong sounded as Mary finished fastening the clasp on Clara's bracelet and Clara froze. It was time to join the others and

Hugh for dinner. Every doubt she'd ever had about stepping away from the wall at balls during her Season rushed back to her, making her want to undress and plead a headache to avoid going down. Except she couldn't be so cowardly. Whatever awaited her at dinner tonight she must face with the same fortitude as she'd met other difficulties. She threw one last look at herself in the mirror, determined to be again a woman worthy of notice by everyone, especially Hugh.

Hugh stood at the bottom of the stairs while the other guests formed up on the steps behind him. He adjusted his cravat and his shirtsleeves for the hundredth time since coming downstairs. After he'd taken leave of Clara at the end of the scavenger hunt, Hugh had done everything he could to distract himself from thinking about her. He'd sought out Lord Tillman to ask his advice about the case facing Everburgh. He'd played billiards with Lord Missington and accepted Lord Wortley's effusive thanks for the brandy which, judging by the high flush on the youth's cheeks, he and Lady Pariston had decided to enjoy the moment the scavenger-hunt party had dispersed. Hugh had then gone to his room to correspond with his man of affairs about Sir Nathaniel's referral and the suggestions Lord Tillman had made. All these things had distracted Hugh for a while, but none of them had kept thoughts of Clara completely at bay.

During the hunt, she'd lived up to her promise to enjoy herself with him, casting no more disparaging remarks at him and even looking on him with admiration when he'd admitted to giving the win to Lady Pariston. That look had meant more to Hugh than the sultry pouts of any of the actresses he'd ever had on his arm, any race he'd ever made in Rotten Row and even the winning shot in the duel with Lord Cecil. It had told him that he could change, that he could be a better man again because she was beginning to see him as one. It hadn't been his goal in giving the win to Lady Pariston to garner Clara's admiration. He'd simply wanted to make an old woman and a young lord who deserved to enjoy the season as much as anyone happy. He knew what it was like to be left behind and forgotten because of poverty or a myriad of other reasons. It's why he'd always liked Adam and his family. Whenever he'd stayed with the Extons during school holidays, they'd never made him feel poor or pitied for his predicament of coming from a distinguished line and not having a pot to piss in. He'd wanted to return a measure of the kindness he'd received where he could. Until this weekend, chances had eluded him, as had the look of admiration Clara had offered him. For a moment, it had taken him back six years, before Lord Matthews's letter had arrived, before his mistakes in London, when every possibility of being happy with Clara had still been real and obtainable. The glimmer that it might be again had lingered in her proud smile and the feeling had been difficult to shake. It was also a dangerous one to entertain.

There couldn't be more between them, especially not while they were under the same roof. Everyone here probably knew about his relationship with Lady Frances and they probably looked on Clara as soon sharing the same predicament, but she wouldn't. She would be no man's mistress, especially not Hugh's, for he wouldn't blot her reputation in such a way nor would he leave this party with her an object of pity like he had before. She didn't deserve such shabby treatment or a tarnished man like Hugh. Even if, like Adam, she could look past all his faults, the past still stood between them, along with Hugh's current financial difficulties. Affection could not bloom beneath the weight of doubts about him and his motives for pursuing her.

The shuffling of feet on the stairs behind him drew Hugh out of his thoughts and he turned to see the guests parting as Clara descended. The earrings dangling from her ears sparkled in the candlelight of the entrance-hall chandelier and glistened against the smooth skin of her neck above the round mounds of her breasts. The rich, deep red silk of her dress heightened the paleness of her skin and brought out the darker tones in her hair. She held her head high with a self-possession to make his chest and other places constrict and nodded like a queen to everyone who greeted her. He couldn't take his eyes off her, especially when she turned her smile on him and she appeared to glow even brighter. Last night, she'd viewed being beside him with all the derision that he'd thrown at duty after Hermione's death, but not tonight. More than one of the gentlemen she passed admired her figure and Hugh's chest filled with pride. She was coming to stand beside him and lead them into the dining room.

Except she wasn't his Marchioness and she carried another man's name.

Regret gripped him as hard as desire. If things had been different six years ago, then she would be here tonight as his wife, with their children in the nursery, the two of them free to enjoy one another's company at dinner and for as many hours afterwards as they wished in the darkness of his room, but that wasn't the way things had ended. Hugh had made another choice and it had cost him any chance of ever having her.

He let out a long breath when she stepped down off the final step and came to stand beside him and laid her gloved hand on his arm. Her touch was light but powerful, making the manor and the other guests fade away. He was proud to give her the sturdiness of his support even if she didn't need it. It was, as the glittering diamonds encircling her neck and rising and falling with each of her long breaths reminded him, the only thing he could offer her. He could not adorn her with dresses and jewellery or even provide her with a house to manage that wasn't plagued by troubles or threatened with ruin. He couldn't even offer her a title. Where precedence and the fate of the name drawing had brought her close to him, reality placed her far beyond his reach. He cursed again his weak and debauched grandfather and all the troubles he'd left for Hugh to correct. The most he could do was enjoy this moment and the brief time that Clara was in his presence.

'You look stunning tonight.' He laid his other hand on top of hers, encasing it in warmth against the chilliness of the main hall. A blush spread across the bridge of her nose and the spattering of freckles marring the fine white skin, adding to her loveliness more than any of the jewels or even the fancy combs in her hair. It reminded him that she was still, in many ways, the Clara he'd first fallen in love with even if he was no longer the Hugh who had captured her heart.

'You're quite striking, too.' She tilted her head a touch to look at him from the corner of her eyes, a teasing smile drawing up the fullness of her cheeks. 'I think your London tailor suits you very well.'

London was not a place he wished to think of right now. 'This isn't from London, but from a local man in the village. I do my best to give him as much work as I can. With Everburgh slowly recovering, I must share with those on my estate what little prosperity we've enjoyed these last few years.'

'But isn't it the fashion to shop in Jermyn Street? You wouldn't want society to consider you unfashionable,' she teased, but there was admiration behind her merriment and he wanted more of it than even the prosperity of his manor, to believe that there might be something more potent between them than this tenuous friendship, a chance to reclaim not just his past reputation but his worthiness to pursue her.

'I don't care what society thinks of me as long as I'm helping those in my care to thrive.'

'Is that really the only time you don't care?' she asked with disbelief.

He could almost hear her thinking the same thing so many matrons did when they spied him—a cross between wanting to protect their daughters from the rumours they'd heard about him and their desire to believe that they weren't true because it better suited their pursuit of a marquess. Except it wasn't a title or his lands that Clara sought, but a man of trustworthiness and honesty. Not for the first time in the last few months he cursed having been so flippant with his reputation. 'It is.'

'What about at the gambling tables?' she asked with a much prettier tone of reprimand than his mother used to employ. She used to scold him like the devil whenever he saw her, afraid he was going down the same path as his grandfather and wanting to stop him, but she hadn't been able to. That decision had needed to come from Hugh. That it had come too late for his mother to witness was another regret to add to the pile.

'I don't gamble.' It was the one vice not even he, in his disgust with the world and fate, could not lower himself to indulge in. He was angry at duty and how all the things he'd been taught to believe in had failed him, but he wasn't a sadistic fool. He wouldn't allow that weakness to erode the few gains that doing his duty had provided or prove beyond a doubt to everyone, and especially himself, that he was as bad a wastrel as his grandfather. Even in his darkest moments he'd held on to the pride of knowing that he was nothing like that man.

'Then when you enjoy your claret at the club?' she prodded.

Sadly, this hit a touch too close to the mark for he'd out drunk more than one lord, winning a considerable sum in a challenge once for being able to remain upright long after his opponent had collapsed on to the floor. It was another victory in which Hugh had taken no real pride, especially when his opponent had become so sick there were fears he would expire from his excesses. Guilt and shame washed over Hugh. For a time, he'd been an ugly man, but he couldn't change it, he could only strive to redeem himself. 'At one time I indulged at my club, but not any more. I've given up drink. I've seen the damage it can do and no longer have a taste for it.'

'Then I commend you for your admirable changes.'

She wouldn't commend him if she knew half of what he'd done, but she didn't and for the moment he could enjoy her tender smile and bask in her approval, no matter how brief it might be.

* * *

The invitation to proceed into the dining room was made and Clara tightened her hold on Hugh's arm, conscious of the thickness of the muscle beneath his fine wool coat. Together they strode into the red-wallpapered room, the walk giving her a chance to consider everything he'd told her. She wanted to believe in the good in Hugh, to trust what she'd seen of him today, but it was hard. During her first and only Season in London, she'd learned that what a man said wasn't as important as what he did. Hugh might speak well of helping those he cared about, but he'd all but turned his back on those in his care when he'd gone dissolute in London. He might have been on the verge once of asking for her hand, but he'd walked away in an instant to marry a richer woman. These actions spoke louder than any of his words, and yet with each strong stride he took beside her, the patient way he waited for her to take the seat next to him before taking his, and the many smiles he brushed her with that she couldn't help but meet, she grew more and more confused about what to think of him.

She flicked out her napkin and set it over

her lap while the footman slid in between them and filled her wine glass before moving on to fill Hugh's. Clara watched Hugh out of the corner of her eye, wondering if he would ignore the drink or if his having sworn off spirits had been a lie intended to bring him further into her good graces. She shouldn't be watching him or concerning herself with his habits. They were none of her business, but she couldn't help herself. Life in the country had become very boring indeed if, in the middle of a lively dinner, this was how she chose to amuse herself.

When Lord Tillman gave a toast to Lord Wortley and Lady Pariston, Clara raised her glass, unable to stop herself from checking to see if Hugh reached for his. He didn't take up the wine, but chose instead the orange juice that had also been provided. Even after the footmen took away the fish and set down the meat, then went around the table with the red wine, leaning past Hugh to fill his glass, it remained on the table in front of him to turn to vinegar in the same way the white had been left. He didn't even appear to notice nor reach for it before jerking back his hand in remembrance of what he'd told her about abstaining.

When Lord Wortley, obviously under the influence of the brandy he'd won and the wine served at dinner, made a toast to their host, everyone took up their glasses again. Clara watched Hugh, waiting to see if he would slip, but again he raised his orange juice glass and, feeling her watching him, furrowed his brow at her in curiosity.

Clara smiled nervously, guilty about trying to catch him out. She shouldn't be so petty and want him to fail, but wish for him to succeed in bettering himself in the same way she was trying to improve herself. He had a great many sins to atone for, but at least he was trying.

'Are you enjoying your orange juice?' she asked.

'I am.' He tilted his glass to her. 'Are you not having any?'

'I will have some, along with a little bit of a confession.' She dropped her voice so as not to be heard by the others.

'I'm listening.' He set down his orange juice and took up his knife and fork, listing a touch towards her to hear what she had to say while he cut his mutton. 'What sins have you committed that I need to hear about?'

She pushed her meat through the gravy on her plate, certain he wouldn't care to listen to her sins as much as she would like to hear some of his. They were probably more interesting and a touch less embarrassing, at least for her. She was only revealing this because she wanted to stop herself from being so petty and for acting like a woman who had nothing more to occupy her time than chewing over old slights. It was the sort of thing a country mouse would do. 'I've been wrong in regards to my opinion of you.'

He paused in the cutting of his mutton and stared at his plate for what felt like ages before he finished slicing through his meat. She waited for him to turn hard eyes on her and for the stony silence that had settled between them last night to return, but it didn't.

'Wrong in what regards?' It was the same tone her mother used to employ when waiting for Clara to tell her the truth about why a particular vase was broken or one of the slices of cake was missing at tea time.

Clara took a deep breath, hesitant to be so honest, but it was more for herself than him, a way to finally let go. 'About the man I thought you'd become since the last time we knew one another. I have not been entirely correct in my assumptions about you.'

He slipped a piece of mutton into his mouth and chewed it for a long while, leaving her to wonder about his response. If someone had frankly told her about their low opinion of her she wouldn't react with this much patience, but snarl at them the way she had Lady Fulton. Hugh did neither, but set down his knife and fork and fingered the stem of his orange-juice glass before finally answering. 'No, you weren't wrong. I was that man deserving of your low opinion. I still am for the way I behaved in London and with you.'

'Why did you court me when you knew you couldn't?' Clara asked without thinking, wanting the answer to the old question, the one that had cast her value as a desired woman into doubt, despite even Alfred's attention and love. She would not live with that lingering doubt any longer.

Hugh glanced down the table to where Anne watched them before a question from Lord Tillman drew her attention away. His voice was barely above a whisper when he answered. 'I never thought the negotiations with Lord Matthews would come to anything.

I thought I was free to follow my heart, but I wasn't.'

'Yes, you were, until you decided you weren't.' She checked her irritation, lowering her voice to match his and keep the conversation discreet between them. She shouldn't be looking back or allowing the old wound to smart so much, but with Hugh and the truth laid out before her like the table settings it was difficult not to confront.

Hugh smoothed his napkin over his lap. 'I've never been free, Clara, not in the way you and Adam are, unaware of what it's like to struggle, to wonder if there will be food on the table, heat or even a roof over your head, to watch your parents ruin their health while they work to free themselves and the estate of crippling debt and court cases.'

'But I had money.'

'Not enough and the debts would have taken it all. I would have dragged you down into poverty with me, ensuring that the suffering and hardship my family endured for twenty years would be visited upon you and our children. I don't want my sons growing up with a great title and threadbare clothes like I did, to see them cold in the winter and hungry every time the harvest failed, to have everything their station should allow them to enjoy sit just beyond their reach and me unable to do anything about it. I saw what that regret did to my parents and I couldn't do that to you or to any future children.' He took a deep breath, staring at the delicate check pattern in the tablecloth while he continued. 'My parents made so many sacrifices for me that when I inherited the estate, I wanted nothing more than to give my mother an easier life free from worry so that her last years would be a comfort instead of a struggle. With a single church ceremony, I was able to do that. You're right. I shouldn't have courted you, but I was young and inexperienced in the way of things and while we were here together I couldn't see the potential consequences, only you and how happy we were together.'

Clara studied him, his face soft with his sincerity and the unspoken desire for her to understand. In his eyes, she caught the faint reflection of the moment he'd stood across from her in the library six years ago. She'd expected a marriage proposal and he'd told her that he was leaving to marry another. The memory didn't burn like it used to because she finally understood why he'd behaved as he had. With her, he'd enjoyed a respite from his crushing responsibilities in the same way she'd enjoyed one from her crippling shyness. Reality had stepped in to end it like it sometimes does. The blame she'd held against him so long finally eased. Adam was right, Hugh had possessed good reasons for marrying another. 'If I'd been in your shoes and seen my mother suffering the way yours had, I would have done the same thing.'

'I appreciate your graciousness. It is a quality most people don't possess.'

'Then it's a good thing you're sitting beside me and not Lady Fulton.' She smiled at him, easing the tension and seriousness between them.

'It is a good thing indeed.' He leaned close to her again, the tang of his shaving soap as tantalising as the glimpse of his thigh clad in tan breeches just beneath the white tablecloth edge. 'Do you remember when Adam and I hid a frog under the silver serving cover for the cook to bring in?'

Clara giggled, trying not to draw attention to them. She'd quite forgotten about that prank and was surprised he'd remembered it. Adam and Hugh had been so young, then, and she even smaller. It was a delight to have someone besides Adam to remember what it had been like at Winsome when her parents had been alive and she'd been a child. 'It was your first visit with us. I was certain Father would never allow Adam to ask you back, but I was wrong. Do you remember when the three of us stole into the kitchen to sneak slices of the plum pudding, the special one our cook had made for the vicar's visit?'

'I do, especially the stern lecture about stealing we got from the vicar after dinner. The man could talk up a storm, couldn't he?'

'He still can. I once caught him warning James and Lillie and a few of their friends with that tale. We are legends in the parish.'

Hugh stifled a large laugh with the back of his hand and Clara was sorry he did. She wanted to hear him laugh like he used to and not appear so trodden on by the world but light and full of hope as he'd been six Christmases ago.

'Do you think your niece and nephew will be able to accomplish such legendary mischief?'

'They try every day to outdo us. One of these days I'm sure they will succeed.'

'I hope not in too many regards, but something worthy of giving your vicar a new story to tell.'

'You will have to help them devise something the next time you come to visit.'

He set down his knife and fork and turned to her. 'Do you think I will be invited to Winsome again?'

There was no mistaking the hope in his question, one she felt deep inside herself. 'Adam likes you, I'm sure you can expect an invitation.'

He straightened one of the forks beside his plate so it matched the other one. 'And would you welcome me to your home?'

Clara took up her wine and indulged in a bracing sip. He cared about whether or not she wanted him at Winsome and, at this moment, she did want him there. It would be like old times with her, Hugh and Adam and it would bring a touch of gaiety to what were sometimes much too serious days. 'I would be happy to have you visit again.'

If Hugh could have taken her hand and pressed his lips to it to convey his gratitude in the most potent way possible he would have, but in the presence of the others he showed restraint. In Clara's words there hadn't been the all-encompassing forgiveness Hugh had been searching for since leaving London, but it was a start. If Clara could absolve him enough to imagine spending more time with him at Winsome, especially after his great mistake with her the last time they were here, there was hope in a complete transformation of himself and his reputation.

'And what will you do now that you've officially returned to society?' Hugh asked, eager for the light conversation they'd enjoyed before, the one that had lifted his spirits. He was also curious about Clara. At one time he'd known her so well, but they'd since become strangers and he no longer wanted it to be like that. He'd experienced and collected enough of those types of people in his life in London. He wanted another real and true friend.

'I don't know.' She cut her meat, her interest in the food fading as she pondered how to answer. 'That's a question I've both considered and avoided for some time. I've never cared much for London.'

'You're right not to.'

'But it's where people are and I need to be

around more people, not alone in the country. Perhaps then I might find someone like Alfred, a good decent man and with him my own place in the world again. I'm too young to be a dowager.'

Hugh tightened his hand on his fork, the jealousy rising up in him at the mention of this unnamed man she sought taking him by surprise. The confidence she'd gained in the last six years added to her beauty more than the inherited jewels or her fine London attire. With such a striking combination, it would only be a matter of time before some man took notice of her and won her hand. Hugh didn't look forward to that day any more than he'd enjoyed hearing of her engagement to Lord Kingston in the months before his own wedding. Back then there'd been the slightest hope of things not working out with Hermione. He'd imagined returning to Clara to try to win her back, but her marriage had put paid to that fantasy. It could happen again and this troubled him more than it should have. 'You won't find a man like him in London.'

'Surely a few gentlemen of quality must venture to town to take up their places in the

House of Lords. Perhaps if I haunt those halls I might find one.'

'Or find yourself installed in a seat and voting for a bill,' he teased, releasing his grip on the silverware. At present there was no other man, simply her and him together at this table. 'If you're especially talented at haunting, no one will even notice that you're there.'

Clara laughed. 'I think my choice of clothing might give me away.'

'Not if you sit high up in the back benches where the less civic-minded lords sleep and simply call out "yea" or "nay" when required. Of course you will have to deepen your voice a touch to make it convincing and not call out too loudly and wake the snoring lord beside you. If you do, smile prettily at him and tell him that you've lost your way to the ladies' gallery.'

'If I startle a lord awake and dazzle him with a look or two, maybe I'll catch a husband.'

He leaned even closer to her, wishing he'd taken his duties in the House of Lord a touch more seriously. 'You wouldn't be the first to do so.'

'Are you saying you've woken up in the House of Lords beside a charming woman before?'

'Not me, but Lord Missington.' He nodded down the table to where the baron and his wife sat together. Lord Missington was a good many years older than the pretty young Lady Missington, but judging by the way they spoke to one another while they ate, appearing quite content in one another's presence, it was obviously a happy marriage.

'Really?' Clara didn't bother to hide her interest in this harmless bit of gossip.

'Yes, except it wasn't in the House of Lords, but at the theatre. He fell asleep in his box and she happened in and sat down, thinking it the box of a friend. When he woke she introduced herself and they have not been parted since.'

She took a sip of her wine, smiling around the edges of thc glass at this charming story. 'Then I will definitely keep my eye out for a napping lord or two.'

'In your presence he would have to be napping to miss your beauty.'

She froze halfway to placing the glass back on the table and Hugh braced himself, waiting for a silent or vocal rebuke for being so forward, but she recovered her mirth and set down her wine. 'Then I shall have no trouble succeeding in London.'

He didn't doubt she would. Any man who couldn't see her charm or who didn't pursue her for more reasons than his pocket wasn't worthy of her. If he hadn't taken himself out of the running with all his past mistakes he might be the man to win her, but while he believed in second chances he knew better than to expect too many. At present, her friendship and good regard would have to be enough.

'The next time you return to London, you must be certain to stay awake so some crafty lady doesn't ensnare you.' She nodded past him to Lady Pariston who watched him with interest, then winked at him when he turned to her.

He took Lady Pariston's small, frail hand in his and raised it to his lips. 'She has already enchanted me.'

'Liar.' Lady Pariston batted her other hand at him, but there was no mistaking the twinkle in her aged blue eyes. 'But you may continue to kiss my hand.'

Clara, Hugh and Lady Pariston laughed, drawing the attention of the entire table.

'What is so amusing, Lord Delamare? You must tell us,' Lady Tillman insisted.

Carla stiffened in her chair, waiting with the others to hear what Hugh had to say and curious about how much he would reveal. Certainly Hugh would have the decency to keep their conversation about her sneaking up on a sleeping lord to ensnare him to himself. She didn't wish to appear so desperate for a second husband as to resort to such ridiculous antics.

'I was telling Lady Pariston how taken I am with her.' He raised the older woman's hand in the air between them with a graciousness that made the ladies at the table sigh.

'But I told him he's too old for me and I've decided on a much younger husband instead.' Lady Pariston flashed doe eyes across the table at Lord Wortley, who turned as red as his wine.

To his credit, the young man, despite his embarrassment, recovered himself quickly. 'When I reach my majority, Lady Pariston, I shall be yours.'

The table erupted in laughter and Clara

relaxed, joining in the gaiety and marvelling at how easily Hugh did the same, turning a roguish smile on all the ladies as they called back and forth across the table, claiming their future intendeds. Clara didn't join in, but watched until Lord Tillman noticed that no one was claiming Clara and called across the table to her.

'What do you say, Lady Kingston? Would you be willing to move down the line of precedence for an old man like me?'

She could think of nothing as witty as Lady Pariston had offered, but raised her glass to her host. 'It would be an honour, my lord.'

'No, I think I'll keep her by my side,' Hugh announced. Clara stiffened at the bold declaration that made the entire table go quiet. He'd dared to compliment her beauty before with a sincerity that had touched Clara to the core. She was sure this announcement was only him teasing her like he used to do when he came for visits with Adam, but suddenly she wasn't so sure. Seeming to sense he'd become too serious, he turned back to Lady Pariston. 'But only if Lady Pariston allows it.'

'She can be the wife. I'll be the mistress.' Lady Pariston threw back her head and laughed.

Everyone laughed, too, but there was a noticeable hesitancy to it this time and Clara wasn't certain if it was for the mention of her as Hugh's wife or Lady Pariston's blatant acknowledgement that some men kept mistresses. It was one thing to know about it and quite another to say it out loud at dinner when people might be planning to slip down the corridors tonight. It was a practice Clara didn't approve of for it left a woman open to ruin while the man risked almost nothing. However, given Lady Pariston's age and experience, she was allowed to be bold and daring with her words.

When the awkward laughter died down, Lady Tillman gently shifted the conversation away from matrimony and adultery and to the ball at Holyfield taking place tomorrow night. They would all attend, just as the Holyfield guests would come to Stonedown on Christmas Eve to enjoy the Tillmans' annual ball. While the ladies eagerly discussed what they would wear and the men surmised what refreshment might be served, Hugh leaned close to Clara once again.

'I hope I didn't offend you with my jokes, but I enjoy us being at the top of the stairs. It gives Lady Fulton a much better view of your diamonds.'

'I agree.' She accepted his kind words the way Lady Pariston had accepted his teasing, doing her best to take it for nothing more than good fun despite the way it made her heart flutter. She'd intended to be friendly with him, but she hadn't imagined sharing more confidences, laughing so easily or enjoying herself this much with him. She could kid herself all night about not caring about him, but she did. It was difficult not to after everything he'd told her and all that they'd shared.

'Good, because you deserve to be at the head of the line where everyone can see you instead of hidden in the middle where you used to be. Don't allow anyone to make you feel inferior.'

Clara sobered and studied his intense brown eyes. There was nothing dishonest about the comment, but a genuine willingness to build her up as she'd tried to do with him at the sundial. It was the same way he'd spoken to her six years ago, helping her to feel more like the daughter and sister of a viscount instead of the country mouse Lady Fulton wanted her to be. She wasn't that woman any more, nor was he the heartless rogue she'd believed him to be. He was Hugh Almstead, Marquess of Delamare, her and her brother's friend. 'Thank you for your appreciation of my place.'

The seriousness between them passed as quickly as it had come and his expression changed to one of delightful enjoyment tinged with humbleness. 'And thank you for putting up with my jokes and for being my partner. I realise I probably wasn't your first choice.'

'If I'd known you were going to give away the brandy, you wouldn't have been.'

He smiled even wider, increasing the quick pace of her heart. Yes, she regretted being paired with him not because of the past and what had happened, but because of the real risk to her heart and her wits. If she reacted so easily to his smiles and tender words, then she was very much in danger of offering Hugh more than her friendship in another moment of honesty between them. Surprisingly, she didn't care. At present, she wanted to be bold like Lady Pariston and less like the reserved Lady Clara Kingston, to laugh and enjoy herself, especially with Hugh.

The men didn't linger long after dinner over their brandy, choosing instead to join the women much sooner. Hugh was glad, for his mood was buoyant after his time with Clara at dinner. He craved more of her fresh humour, the lilting notes of her voice and the optimism in her manner. It was something that had been sorely lacking in the ladies of London, especially with Lady Frances and the hours he'd wiled away with her more out of boredom than desire.

The moment he entered the sitting room, he spied Clara on the sofa near the fireplace. Unlike many of the other women who were at the tables playing cards, she sat alone, watching the logs burn, the warm firelight caressing her face. She'd chosen to stay up tonight instead of retreating to her room as she had last night and he knew that she was waiting for him.

Hugh fought the urge to rush over and sit beside her, choking on the formality required by all the people gathered here. While he made his way slowly around the room, he remained as aware of Clara's presence as he was certain she was of his. Many of the men took places at the card tables, but Hugh didn't despite the numerous invitations to join various games. Instead, he stopped here and there to watch others play and to help poor Lord Wortley to win a hand by pointing out that he had four eights.

Finally, when he reached the table closest to hers, he extricated himself from Lady Fulton's desire to hear some news of London and sat beside Clara.

'I thought for sure Lady Fulton would trap you at the table and make you tell her every detail of the last theatre performance you attended.' Clara peered up at him through her lashes, the gesture as beguiling as her unashamed confession that she'd followed his progress around the room. With her rich eyes fixed on his and the rainbows from her gems splashing over her neck and cheeks, his reservation and reasons against pursuing her began to vanish. Could they start over?

Hugh shifted on the sofa, the question pricking him like an errant feather from the down cushions. At one time he'd wanted nothing more than to win her back, but that time had passed after her marriage and his. Yet here they were, choosing to sit together and speak the same way they'd done six years ago, as easy with one another as they'd been during all his visits to Winsome. 'She isn't charming enough to trap me and the last play I saw wasn't good enough to relate in detail to anyone, including the audience.'

'Do you intend to give up the temping delights of London for good?' Clara asked, her pretty voice as warming as the fire in the grate.

'I had planned to avoid town for a couple of Seasons, but with this new matter facing Everburgh, I'll have to return with the opening of Parliament in the spring. It will stop me from fulfilling my vow to give up less reputable establishments.'

Her smile faltered a touch. 'You mean clubs and other places?'

He tilted towards her, her full lips slightly parted as enticing as her sweet perfume. 'I mean the House of Lords and most government offices.'

She laughed, the sound as charming as the

sight of Lord and Lady Missington together in the window seat, still smitten with each other after a number of years of marriage. 'Adam never makes sitting in the House of Lords sound so delicious.'

'Then press him to tell you better stories than whatever he's telling you now.'

'I must. It also gives me even more reason to return to London with him and Anne in the spring. I want to see all of these things you've described tonight.'

'I only hope I haven't built them up so much that you find them disappointing.'

'After the quiet of the country, any spectacle in London, no matter how disappointing, will be a nice change.'

Hugh tapped his knee, considering his words before he spoke. 'Perhaps I can join you on a few of these excursions? I imagine this Season's theatre bill must be better than last Season's and I'd hate to disappoint the next person who asks me to describe a performance.'

'I think, given your and Adam's friendship, it's very likely you will accompany us,' she answered, as non-committal as he was hesitant. 'You must tell me what other dens of vice to visit, such as the Royal Academy and the British Museum.'

'The British Museum is the worse. You shouldn't go there. More people meet scandalously in the Greek Gallery than at the theatre. It's awful.' He shook his head in mock disapproval, this chance to deride London as pleasurable as strolling beside her and listening to the silk of her dress rustle against her legs. She was lovely here beside him, back straight, shoulders firm, and her gems adding to her beauty instead of making up for a lack of it. She didn't need them or any fancy airs to be stunning, but he enjoyed them all the same.

'And what of Vauxhall? I've heard wicked things about what takes place along the dark paths there.'

'It's a nunnery compared to Hookham's. The people perusing their prints will taint any respectable woman.'

She crossed her hands in her laps in decision. 'Then I must go there for I'm in desperate need of a new novel to read.'

'Make sure it is a very bad one for you want to keep up with the latest fashion.'

'I'll make sure it is one of the worst,' she assured him with a wink.

It was then Hugh happened to notice the interest that Lord Westbook took in their conversation. He sat on the far side of the card table closest to them, deep in conversation with Lady Fulton who sat on his left. While they spoke, Lord Westbook took in Hugh with a scrutiny that Hugh would have demanded Lord Westbook explain if they were in his club in St. James's. Here, he allowed the overly curious and condemning look to stand, not wanting to create any more trouble for Clara than he might have already caused by sitting beside her longer than precedence and dinner demanded.

If she was aware of Lord Westbook's interest in them, she made no indication of it, taking in instead the selection of rich desserts laid out on the table in front of them by a footman in the Tillmans' blue and gold livery. One could always count on indulging at Stonedown.

'You're not having any?' Clara noticed he didn't make a move for the food while she selected a plate along with a few tempting treats.

Hugh glanced at her, then the assortment and then Lord Westbook, catching him and Lady Fulton watching both Hugh and Clara from the corners of their eyes. As much as he wished to stay here and enjoy a custard along with more of Clara, he suspected it was time for him to leave. They'd made a great deal of progress today. He was loath to have a bunch of busybodies ruin it.

'I don't think I will. In fact, it's time for me to retire.'

'Already?' She gasped with no small amount of genuine surprise. 'What would people in London say if they saw you going to bed before midnight?'

'That I'm preparing for a dawn duel.' This made her smile again, the sight of it warming him more than the raging fire in the grate. 'Goodnight, Lady Kingston.'

To his silent delight, disappointment at losing his company whispered across her face. 'Goodnight, Lord Delamare.'

He didn't rise, but continued to regard her as she did him, and the room and all the people surrounding them seemed to disappear. If he touched his lips to hers, she would raise her hand to his cheek, press herself against him and surrender to the need flooding them both. It was there in her wide eyes and parted lips, in the way she leaned forward on the one hand, resting on the brocade between them, and tilted her head up to him, inviting him to come closer. If he did, she would be his again. All he need do was slide over and press his hip against hers as he slid his arm around her back. He laid his hand on the cushion, his fingertips achingly close to hers, every muscle in his body tight with the desire to touch her, but he didn't move. He couldn't. They weren't alone.

Instead, he pulled his hand away and rose, offering her a bow, a temporary farewell before turning and denying himself the sight of her. With each step that carried him away from her, he fought the urge to return by reminding himself that there was tomorrow and more time. He would not make the same mistakc as before and rush at her like some starstruck boy. Instead, he would employ patience like a proper gentleman. With her taking her first steps back into society after the seclusion of her widowhood, he didn't wish to command all her attention, but to give her a chance to decide and choose, and himself a chance to prove that he deserved her affection and attention. The spark of something had flared between them and there was plenty of time to coax it into roaring fire, assuming it didn't find a reason to flare out.

Clara watched Hugh go, missing his humour and companionship before he'd even stepped out of the door. For a little while tonight, the boy she'd known at Winsome, the one she'd fallen in love with at Stonedown had been beside her. With him, she'd felt a little more like the carefree young woman she'd once been and not the mourning matron. Without him, the unease that his conversation and teasing had kept at bay slowly began to return. She glanced at the cushion and the imprint of his hand lingering there and traced it with one finger, making the feathers beneath the fabric shift until the outline and the warmth of him began to fade. What remained was the craving for Hugh that had enveloped her when they'd sat so close. There'd been more than friendship in his eyes when she'd thought he would lean forward and take her hand and kiss her.

Kiss me, indeed. She smoothed what remained of the imprint out of the cushion and sat up straight. He wasn't about to be so bold in a room full of people, nor would she have allowed it, except she would have. Apparently, she'd been without a man for too long if she were so eager to kiss the first one who showed any interest in her. Lady Pariston would say there was only one remedy for it, but Clara feared the cure would be worse than the illness and she wasn't about to throw away any chance of proving that she'd changed by potentially making the same mistake twice. Only she wondered if the mistake was in letting Hugh go.

She looked at the door where he'd disappeared through, tempted to rise and go after him when movement along the edge of her vision made her turn. Anne, who couldn't hide her delight behind her hand of cards, was watching her, as was Lady Pariston, who nodded with approval. However, it was Lady Fulton's smug smile and Lord Westbook's scrutiny that jerked Clara out of her daydreams and back into the sitting room.

She was doing it again, being careless in her regard for Hugh in front of everyone and risking another public humiliation.

He wouldn't do that to me again, or would he? She didn't know. Whoever he'd been in London, that man was not the one she'd been with during the scavenger hunt or at dinner or just now, but the London one remained behind him like a shadow, clouding her view of him.

There's no reason to rush into any decision, either for or against him, she reminded herself, rising to join one of the card games and to stop everyone from staring at her and speculating. She would keep her before-dinner vow to be careful and watch and observe him, to have the patience to draw out the truth about Hugh, good or bad. Her mind hoped it would be bad and then she could walk away proud of herself for having avoided any pitfalls, but her heart had other ideas, ones she was afraid to admit even to herself.

Chapter Six

Thick shafts of morning sunlight streamed in through the large windows lining the upstairs hall of Stonedown Manor. Clara moved through each of these warm patches, ignoring the magnificent views of the winter countryside surrounding the manor outside. She held on tight to the banister while she descended the stairs, far more awake than expected after a night spent tossing and turning while she worked to untangle the mess of thoughts she held about Hugh until, exhausted by the effort, she'd finally fallen asleep. The bliss of unconsciousness had been short lived and she'd awakened long before sunrise to mull over again all the things discussed yesterday. She'd forced herself to stay in bed until the sun had at last peeked through the heavy curtains and the maid had entered to light the fire. Then she'd taken her time dressing, all the while trying to pretend that she didn't want to hurry downstairs and see Hugh again. She'd dreaded her first morning here and encountering him. This morning, she longed for more laughter and jokes and the excitement of whatever the Tillmans had planned. This wasn't at all how she wished to be. She wanted to be rational and calm, cool headed and logical where Hugh was concerned, and she was being everything but. Even now when it should make no difference to her whether he was below stairs or still in his room she had to struggle not to race to the dining room and see if he was there and how things might be between them today.

As she approached the dining room, she forced her racing heart to still with each step that drew her closer to breakfast and possibly Hugh. She didn't wish to walk in and beam at him like the smitten ten-year-old who'd followed him around Winsome during his first visit, her head full of fanciful dreams that he might notice her. She was too refined a lady to behave like that, although at times last night she'd wondered if she was as refined as she believed. When he'd sat with her on the sofa she'd felt very much like that smitten ten-year-old and had almost behaved like one.

Blast all this nonsense. She paused at the dining-room door, pushed back her shoulders and strode in like a marchioness.

The instant she crossed the threshold she realised how futile worrying about Hugh had been. He wasn't there. None of the men were present except for Lord Westbook, who sat at the far end of the table beside Lady Fulton enjoying his eggs and ham. It was a stark reminder of why Clara shouldn't allow herself to be carried away when it came to Hugh. If he was half as excited to see her as she'd been to see him he would have been here waiting for her.

Shoving down her disappointment, Clara offered greetings to those seated at the table before making her way to the sideboard, far more reserved in her movements than she'd been before she'd entered, but no less agitated. She looked over the selection of food in the chafing dishes, but her stomach was too knotted for her to choose more than a slice of toast. She should be glad that Hugh wasn't here for it spared her the effort of being in the same room with him and pretending at indifference. She wished she really was indifferent. She was tired of her emotions bouncing around like an overeager puppy.

'Ah, Lady Kingston, good morning.' Lord Westbook stepped up beside her at the sideboard and refilled his plate. It was amazing he was so slender given how much food he ate. 'Come and sit with me for a while. It's been ages since we've spoken.'

He wasn't exactly the man she wished to speak to this morning, or any morning for that matter, and she cast him a sideways glance, wondering why he was suddenly so interested in her and why he was the only man in the dining room. 'Where are the rest of the gentlemen?'

She could guess why he was interested in her.

'They decided to take advantage of the morning sun to enjoy a ride. Most don't think the good weather will last and we'll have snow by Christmas. Not being much of a rider myself, I decided to remain indoors.'

This gave Clara a touch of hope as she set her plate at an empty seat at the table and waited for the footman to pull out her chair. If all the gentlemen were eager to ride, Hugh couldn't have been expected to remain behind with the ladies like Lord Westbook. She would see him again shortly, for the men were sure to return before the end of breakfast to fortify themselves for whatever event Lord and Lady Tillman had planned next. Clara sat down, amazed when Lord Westbook took the open place beside her. Lady Fulton was still at the table and would make him a better dining partner than Clara.

'How are you finding Lord Delamare? Is your pairing successful?' he asked, leaning too far over the arm of the chair and taking much more interest in her answer than politeness dictated.

'It is going well.' She scraped some butter over her toast, littering the china with crumbs. 'And your pairing with Lady Fulton?'

'Splendid, of course.' He flicked his hand as if waving away a fly, making it clear it was not his pairing he wished to discuss when he lowered his hand to the arm of his chair and leaned closer, dropping his voice. 'But I'm concerned about you.'

'Are you now?' she answered between bites of her toast, wishing he'd go away.

'I was here during that awful business between the two of you last time when we all thought he would declare for you. How embarrassing it must have been when he left so abruptly and then announced his engagement to Lady Hermione.'

She worked to choke down the dry toast. His desire to make sure she remembered her embarrassment was irritating, especially with Lady Fulton watching them. She resisted the urge to dump her plate of crumbs in his lap and tell him a thing or two about his manners. Instead, she took another bite of toast with all the dainty disregard for him and his comment that she could muster. 'That was a long time ago, Lord Westbook, and I've quite forgotten most of it.'

'Yes, but I fear Lord Delamare may be up to his old games.'

His sugary caring, so different from Hugh's genuine concern, made her stomach twist. 'You have nothing to worry about on my account.'

'But I do. I've known you too long not to be worried, especially with you being a widow—my condolences on your loss.' He laid a long-fingered hand over his heart, his signet ring clinking against one of the buttons on his waistcoat. Clara offered a terse nod in acceptance which gave him leave to continue in his present vein while she tried to contrive some way to politely extricate herself from this conversation.

She glanced across the table to Anne, who'd come in and taken a seat and who watched their exchange with incredulous curiosity. Clara knew the minute she shook free of this troublesome man, Anne would sweep her away to find out what he'd wanted. Good, for she needed a distraction both from thinking of Hugh and fuming over Lord Westbook's insolence.

'I realise that things are more permissible than a number of years ago,' Lord Westbook continued, 'but I want to warn you about indulging in all the delights of a house party. Lord and Lady Tillman, like most hosts, are quite tolerant of, how shall I say it, unorganised nocturnal activities, but it doesn't mean everyone else is.'

Clara dropped the half-eaten toast on her plate, unwilling to endure any more of this insufferable man and all his unwanted and lewd suggestions. 'Lord Westbook, we are not on familiar enough terms for my delight in a house party to be any of your affair.'

She moved to rise, but he placed a staying hand on her arm. 'I don't mean to be rude, Lady Kingston, but if you'd heard the things I have about Lord Delamare, you would be far less congenial to him than you are at present.'

Clara said nothing, curiosity getting the better of her and keeping her in her seat.

Lord Westbook glanced around to make sure no one was listening before he spoke in a low voice, taking her silence for an invitation to continue. 'For a number of months, Lord Delamare was involved with Lady Frances, a young window much like yourself who is well known in London. Despite a great deal of speculation, no marriage proposal was forthcoming when both were free to take their pleasures legally, as one might say, and to protect the future, of, how shall I put it, any consequences of their liaison. He didn't, but broke with her six months ago, casting a serious shadow on her reputation. His reputation did not suffer for with his carrying on with more than a few actresses, much like his grandfather used to do, his behaviour was nothing more than what people expected of him. His one saving grace is not having gone into debt which ruins so many men, but this one admirable trait does not make up for the rest.'

Clara wasn't sure which disgusted her more, hearing his frank discussion of other people's intimate lives or the unpleasant details that Lord Westbook provided about Hugh. She'd heard a number of stories about Hugh, but nothing about him having a mistress. It wouldn't be difficult to discreetly learn whether or not everything he'd told her about Hugh and Lady Frances was real or one of Lord Westbook's exaggerations. Sadly, the sinking in the pit of her stomach practically answered the question for her. She'd left Hugh last night with a greatly raised opinion of him, but it was wilting fast in the face of Lord Westbook's story. It lifted the veil from her eyes and helped her to see the situation as it was not as she wanted it to be. His actions were defining him more than any of his words ever could.

'I'm sorry if what I said upsets you, but I remember your parents with great fondness and I'd hate to see you fall prey again to a man like Lord Delamare,' Lord Westbook explained.

Whatever Lord Westbook's motives for speaking to her, she couldn't remain here, not with Lady Fulton watching them and making heaven knew what of it. Clara could well imagine. She thought Hugh's absence had spared her any difficulties this morning, but instead it had made them far worse.

She set her napkin on the table beside her meagre and half-eaten breakfast, careful to show nothing of the turmoil inside of her as she faced him. 'Thank you for your concern, Lord Westbook, but I assure you I am quite adept at fending off false offers of friendship.'

She rose and this time he didn't stop her. In a daze, she left the room, but instead of going up, she wandered to the library, needing time to think over what he'd said and how she would deal with it. The Hugh that Lord Westbook had described was not the man who'd been with her at the sundial or the one who'd sat beside her at dinner and afterwards and who'd looked on her with an admiration she hadn't seen since she'd walked down the aisle to meet Alfred. He was a gentleman who'd cared only for his own pleasures and concerns in London, heedless of the damage it did to the woman he was with. If she were not careful she might become like that woman, for if Hugh had seen no reason to marry Lady Frances after dallying with her so that all of London was aware of it, then he wasn't likely to offer for Clara should anything develop between them.

Nothing will develop between us, especially not after hearing this news. She had more self-respect than to lower herself in such a manner, especially when Hugh would be free to walk away from her again, especially if any consequences should arise from their liaison. She longed for a child of her own, but she would not make it a bastard.

She paced back and forth across the large rug in the centre of the room, annoyed that her holiday should be plagued by this nonsense. Hugh wasn't why she was here. She wanted to have fun and enjoy herself, not be bogged down in all this fretting and worrying. She'd done enough of that in the days leading up to Alfred's death and afterwards when she'd been bereft of a husband, a place, all her dreams for a family of her own and lost and lonely. Except Hugh had lifted a great deal of that loneliness yesterday and she couldn't help but want more of it, but not if it meant becoming another Lady Frances.

Clara sat down on the leather sofa, the coldness of the material seeping through her gown along with a growing weariness. She should never have allowed Anne to talk her into coming here.

'Clara, are you all right?' Anne entered the library and peered about as if she'd never been in this room before. 'You left breakfast so quickly.'

'I'm fine, only Lord Westbook was making a nuisance of himself.'

'Isn't he always?'

'He outdid himself this morning by warning me to be a little more careful where Lord Delamare was concerned, as if how the two of us regard one another is any of his business. Then he told me something quite shocking.'

'About Lady Frances?'

Clara jumped to her feet in shock. 'You know about her, too, and didn't think to warn me?'

'His past relationship with her has no bearing on the present situation.'

'Of course it does. How am I to form a true opinion of him if I don't have all the facts?' Her sister-in-law could be as bad as Lord Westbook when it came to indulging in other people's affairs, especially Clara's, except this time she hadn't stepped in when it would have been to Clara's advantage for her to do so. She needed to have a conversation with her sister-in-law about sharing *all* the gossip with her, not just some of it.

Anne crossed her arms and slid Clara a sly look. 'A proper opinion? Is that what you're forming with Lord Delamare?'

Clara went to the nearest bookshelf and pulled out a book to flip through, not really caring what it was about. 'There is nothing between us. We were paired up and we are being cordial and friendly with one another.'

'Is that what they call it now?'

'That is exactly what it's called.' Clara shoved the book back into the hole in the bookcase. 'Besides, what am I supposed to do, ignore him?'

'I must be very right for you to be so cross with me.'

'I'm not cross, I simply hate for people to think there is more to it when there isn't.'

And there wasn't, or so she continued to say, but it was clear she wasn't fooling anyone, especially not herself. If he had tried to kiss her last night, she would have allowed it and this troubled her as much as trying to work out Hugh's real character. Oh, but the man was frustratingly perplexing. 'Why are you so interested in me and Lord Delamare? Surely there are better, more eligible men that you and Adam could throw in my path.'

'Not this week, there isn't,' Anne answered as if this were not a very grave subject.

Clara huffed in frustration, forcing Anne to take this discussion a touch more seriously.

She approached Clara with an earnestness that was not very convincing. 'Clara, we are at a house party in the country during Christmas. Other than partaking in the events, speculating about what other guests are up to is almost all there is to do here. You would be doing it, too, if you weren't at the centre of that very speculation.'

Clara took a deep breath. Anne was right. Clara and her mother had attended a number of house parties after her coming out where they'd spent a great deal of time wondering who was pairing with whom. She never thought to be standing here wondering about herself.

'Why not enjoy the attention and the fun?' Anne suggested. 'After all, isn't that's what you came here to do?'

'No, I mean, yes, but not with Hugh.'

Anne cocked a curious eyebrow. 'Hugh?'

'Lord Delamare.' Clara balled her hands in frustration at her slip for it gave a great deal of credence to all Anne's insinuations. 'What do you know of him and Lady Frances?'

This dulled Anne's amusement. 'I've heard that Lord Delamare, like a great number of gentlemen in London, does have something of a past, which as a matron you are allowed to hear about.'

'And the fact that he wouldn't marry her? Am I allowed to hear about that?'

'Lord Westbook has been busy, hasn't he?'

'And he's right, isn't he?'

'I'm sure there's a good reason why Lord Delamare didn't marry Lady Frances although I'm not privy to it. Don't assume the worst of him, Clara. He's had a rough time of things and, like you, he needs friends.'

It wasn't a friend Clara needed, but someone who would cherish her the way she wished to be cherished, to be there for her when she was hurting and to make her smile and laugh and to give her hope. She had her doubts about that man being Hugh.

'Come, we must dress for the next activity,' Anne said.

'Fine.' Clara yanked a book off the shelf without looking at the title, tired of wading through all these roaring thoughts. She followed Anne out into the hallway, not caring what book she carried. She wouldn't be surprised if she climbed into bed tonight to see she'd chosen a tome on the subject of irrigating crops. Oh, well, at least she would learn something.

Anne and Clara were not two feet out of the office when Lady Tillman approached with her hand on a young man's arm. He was new to the party and to Clara, and tall, not as tall as Hugh, but impressive enough with sandy blond hair and light brown eyes. His chin was sharper and not as strong as Hugh's, nor was his chest so well developed beneath his finely tailored suit. The cut of his coat reminded her more of those men whose tailors were firmly established in London than

Hugh's and she sensed at once this was no country gentleman.

'Lady Kingston, Lady Exton, allow me to introduce you to Lord Stanhope. He's a friend of my cousin and is joining us for the remainder of the week. It's his first Christmas house party here at Stonedown.'

'Or any manor, truth be told,' he offered with appealing graciousness.

'Then you're in for a treat, for no one hosts a party so well as Lord and Lady Tillman and you're sure to enjoy tonight's ball at Holyfield. It isn't as good as Lady Tillman's Christmas Eve one, but I'm sure you'll find everyone very welcoming and in good spirits,' Anne offered, doing her best to make the man feel welcome, but with his easy stance and air of confidence, Clara suspected he needed no encouragement to step straight in to any group or festivities and make himself at home.

'The country ladies will be thrilled to have a new dance partner,' Clara added, not as clearheaded as Anne to think of something more witty or interesting to say.

'Might I be so bold as to ask for your first dance, Lady Kingston, before the country ladies overwhelm me?' He shifted the full focus of his charm from Anne to her and, if Clara was not mistaken, it radiated a little brighter for her than it had for her sister-in-law. Over his shoulder, Anne widened her eyes at Clara as if to say there was now someone besides Hugh to be thrown in Clara's path. Clara ignored her, thinking her sister-in-law was the worst matchmaker she'd ever encountered.

Instead, she kept her eyes fixed on Lord Stanhope's, standing up a touch straighter when he dropped his gaze down to take in the length of her before raising it once again to meet hers. 'Yes, it would be a pleasure to enjoy the first dance with you, Lord Stanhope.'

If Hugh had been given half the warnings she'd received today from so-called well-meaning people like Lord Westbook, then he wasn't likely to ask her to dance with him. Good. She didn't need to give anyone any additional reasons to keep speculating on whether or not she would become the next Lady Frances. There was someone new here that they could whisper about, one with no past connection to her and whose presence by her side would cause a great deal less whispering and speculations. Dancing with Lord Stanhope might not have been what she'd imagined for this evening, but he would be a refreshing change from the last day.

'Until tonight, Lady Kingston.' Lord Stanhope offered her a bow worthy of an audience with the King and then allowed Lady Tillman to lead him off to make more introductions, but not before tossing Clara one last look over his shoulder, his smile as strong as his stride.

'I suspect Lord Delamare might have some competition,' Anne joked.

'Lord Delamare doesn't need to worry. His past behaviour has already knocked him out of the running.'

'Clara, don't underestimate the power of a good apology from a man. I have gained some of my best jewellery from Adam this way.' Anne laughed, for she and Adam rarely fought.

'It is probably my jewels more than me he's after.'

'Really, Clara…'

'No, I won't be tricked by him again. Let him woo some other widow, I will see what other men there are in the world.' He wasn't the only one worth having.

Hugh and Adam walked back from the stables, the musky scent of horses and leather saddles clinging to them as much as the cold morning air. When Adam, Sir Nathaniel and some of the others had asked him to ride this morning, he'd quickly agreed. The stinging air and the demands of commanding a horse had been a welcome distraction after a night spent lying on his back, staring up at the ceiling and thinking of Clara. She'd dominated his thoughts more so than even six years ago until he could think of nothing but her, not even the dangers facing Everburgh. It was wrong, but he'd been powerless to stop it. When he and Clara had laughed and reminisced about their past at Winsome, his current troubles had lessened their hold over him. She'd been the girl who'd once captured his heart because she hadn't derided him for having a grand title and no money. When they'd ridden together over the grounds of Stonedown in the sleigh, she'd listened to all his dreams for Everburgh and had believed that they would come true. He hadn't realised he would have to let her go in order for his dreams to be realised. But it was no longer six years ago and his reasons for not pursuing Clara were beginning to fade as quickly as the frost on the grass.

It was how he would win her that had remained as elusive as sleep. The truth was he hadn't had to work for her heart before, their love had simply blossomed. Now a great many obstacles stood between them and he would have to clear each one if he wished to make her his.

'I'm glad to see you and Clara getting along so well,' Adam remarked from beside him as they walked from the stables to the main house.

'We are, surprisingly well.' Hugh's breath formed small clouds above his head before the wind carried them off. 'She told me she's considering venturing to London for the Season.'

'Good. I very much want to see her back out in the world again. It will help for her to have another friend in London.'

'I'd be more than happy to escort her when required, if you and she are amenable to the idea.' Hugh wondered how far he might venture with Clara and if Adam would disapprove or not. Adam knew more about Hugh's past than most and, despite remaining his friend, Hugh wondered if Adam would see him as a suitable match for his sister. She might not need her brother's permission to marry, but her family was important to her and he refused to cause strife between them. Even if Adam did approve, if fate contrived to separate Hugh and Clara again and she was hurt, he was sure Adam would finally discard him and Hugh's quiet re-introduction to society would end. His title might gain him a certain admiration and invitation, but he no longer wished to be a titled face at a ball and to return at night to a silent house. He would rather not be invited to a hundred balls and have one good and true friend and the real love of a wife than to strut about in society with his station and a gaggle of hangers-on who would disappear the moment they got wind of any trouble or difficulty.

'Are you quite free to serve as Clara's escort?' It was a probing question, the kind the father of a potential fiancée might ask.

'I'm entirely free and under no obligations to anyone. Lady Frances and I broke with one another six months ago. I have not spoken to her since nor has she made any effort to contact me.' It'd been a mutual parting with neither of them suffering when the end had finally come. They'd never been in love, merely a convenience. Lady Frances was a shrewd woman who'd been married to a much older man before he'd died and had delighted in the attention of a man her age. She understood the way of the world and was not full of enough dreams and whimsy to wish to bind herself to a lord with a great deal of hard work ahead of him.

'I'm glad to hear it.' Adam clapped Hugh on the back as they climb the stairs to the doors of Stonedown.

Adam and Hugh spoke of possible hunting in the autumn before they parted at the top of the main staircase to go to their rooms to dress. While Hugh prepared for the day, he thought about Clara and how much he wanted to see her again. Whether she was as elated by the prospect of being with him remained to be seen. She'd been friendly and tempted by him last night and it gave him hope, but the light of day and a night to think things over could change things. Either way, he would not be as serious or melancholy with her as he'd been yesterday. Not every connection between them could be about mourning or past troubles, for he was certain there were other, more enjoyable things to draw them together and make the holiday much brighter for both of them.

Chapter Seven

Hugh stood at the back of the guests assembled in small groups and scattered about the main staircase of Stonedown Manor. It'd taken him longer than he would have liked to dress, making him the last to join the group and hear what Lord and Lady Tillman had planned for today.

Hugh peered over everyone's heads, searching for Clara. He spied her on the far side of the group standing beside Lady Exton. The sunlight illuminating the room from the windows flanking the front door played in the wisps of hair escaping from the loose curls at the back of Clara's head. She did not wear the elaborate jewellery that had adorned her last night, but had chosen instead simple pieces of gold with smaller gems that highlighted the lighter colour of her deep yellow gown. Her bright dress was a stark contrast to the more muted colours that she had worn for the last two days and the warmer shade lightened her face, which would have shone even more if she'd worn a smile instead of her strangely strained look.

Her lips were pressed tight together and there was no trace of the ease with which she'd sat beside him last night, nor did she appear as excited about the forthcoming game as the others. In fact, she looked as thrilled as she had when she'd come downstairs on the first night to stand beside him. She also didn't hazard a glance at him although he was certain she was aware that he was here. She was purposely ignoring him the same way she'd done when she'd sat beside him at the first dinner.

Worry crept into Hugh, pushing out the excitement and hope that he'd experienced during the early hours of dawn and in the time since. Something had happened between last night and this morning and it had changed her opinion of him. Then he caught Lord Westbook's eye and the answer seemed to make itself clear in the superior arch of his brow before he turned back to listen to Lord Tillman.

As if unable to avoid Hugh's searching stare, Clara finally glanced in his direction. He smiled and nodded at her, conscious of the thrill that gripped him at capturing this small bit of her attention. The feeling evaporated when she did not return the smile or do anything more than turn back to Lord and Lady Tillman, deliberately snubbing Hugh. If he could have pressed his way through the guests and come to her side and drawn her into another room where they could speak privately he would have, but he wasn't about to make a scene, especially while Lord and Lady Tillman were explaining the next activity.

'With the weather a great deal colder today and with everyone in need of a free afternoon to prepare for the Holyfield ball tonight, we've decided on a game of hide and seek.'

'Rather scandalous, don't you think, Lord Tillman?' Sir Nathaniel called out, as amused as he was serious in his question.

'Given our present pairings, I don't believe we have a reason to worry or to suspect that anyone will be doing too much dallying while the searcher seeks out his quarry.'

A number of people turned to look at either Hugh or Clara and Hugh inwardly groaned. This would not help him make his case against whatever had turned Clara against him this morning.

'Speak for yourself, Lord Tillman.' Lady Pariston laughed, grabbing on tight to Lord Wortley's arm and making everyone laugh, except Clara.

This did not bode well for a pleasant afternoon with her.

'Who will be searching?' Mrs Alton asked.

'Lord Stanhope. Being the newest member of our party, he is without a partner and has graciously agreed to be our searcher.' Lady Tillman motioned to Lord Stanhope who stood off to one side with an air of languid superiority on his square face. Hugh didn't know much of the man, but he didn't like the way he glanced up the stairs at Clara, flashing her a very inviting smile that, to his chagrin, she returned. He wished the Tillmans would hurry up and get on with the game, then he could speak to Clara and find out what was the matter.

'When the gong rings, you'll have five minutes to hide. Then the gong will sound again and Lord Stanhope will begin his search. There is nowhere on this floor in Stonedown that you may not venture, but you are not to go upstairs. The butler is going to stand here to make sure you don't. The prize today will be to lead the first dance at the Holyfield ball tonight.' Lady Tillman motioned to the butler who stood up on the landing with the gong. He rang it and Lady Tillman clapped her hands together before announcing, 'To your hiding places.'

The room quickly emptied as everyone grabbed their partner and set out in search of the perfect place to conceal themselves. Hugh strode through the confusion of people to reach Clara, who appeared in no hurry to set out or to be alone with him.

'Where do you suggest we hide? You know this house better than many and must be privy to all its secret chambers and rooms,' Hugh said, trying to inject some of the spirit of the game into the tense air between them.

'I don't have as intimate a knowledge of the house as you believe so you may choose where we hide.' Her flat tone made it clear that the last thing she wished to do this morning was hide with Hugh waiting for who knew how long to be discovered.

He'd been eager to reach her before, but now he wasn't so certain he wanted to be alone with her and risk her sharp words but he had no choice. He must find out why she'd changed her attitude to him since he'd seen her last night and this was the best way to do it without danger of anyone whispering about them are overhearing. 'I have an idea. Follow me.'

He raised his hand to take hers and then thought better of it. He turned on his heels and led her away from the entrance hall. She followed in silence, as dour as if this was nothing more than another duty that had to be done before she could continue with the rest of her day.

The deeper they walked into the house, the less they heard other people, with the occasional door closing or a muffled giggle to alert them that there were a few souls around them.

'Where are you going?' Clara asked.

'The large cupboard near the billiards room.' Hugh reached the door set in the panelling in the wall just beyond the billiards room, the last one along the long corridor before the large window at the end. He pulled it open to reveal old trays of billiard balls and stands holding extra sticks waiting to be used if a number of guests wished to play at the same time. It was a small, musty room, but wide enough for two people to secrete themselves away for a little while. 'Quick, in here.'

Hugh turned to find Clara standing halfway down the hall.

'You want us to hide in a cupboard?' She threw him a dubious look that he was certain had more to do with the confines of the space and how close they would be forced to stand rather than the actual hiding place itself.

'Lord Stanhope isn't familiar with the house and, if nothing else, it will take him some time to search the other rooms. With any luck, by the time the gong rings he won't have come this far and we'll still be hidden.'

'I don't know if I'd call that lucky,' Clara murmured and Hugh questioned the wisdom of stepping into such tight quarters with this little tiger. He was apt to be bit, but if he didn't take the chance he might not discover what was troubling her.

Thankfully, the deep sound of the gong marking the start of the game made her dart into the small space faster than any words he could think of to convince her to join him. He followed her inside, closing the door behind him.

While Hugh's eyes adjusted to the dim light filtering in from beneath the door, he listened to Clara's quick breaths, noting how they slowed as she settled herself in the darkness and waited with him to either be found or to have to reveal themselves at the end of the game. Hugh guessed she was praying they would be discovered quickly, for there were no words about winning and becoming the lead couple in the first dance and showing up people like Lady Fulton and Lord Westbook. There was only a silence as tortuous as her rose perfume. The scent of it was more potent than the dust covering the equipment and he longed to break the tension between them by reaching out and slipping his arm around her waist. He could draw her to him and bury his face in the curve of her neck and inhale the sweet warmth of her skin, leave small kisses in the hollow of her throat and make her sigh with a pleasure to drive out all her objections to him, but Hugh didn't move. He could see in the faint light slipping beneath the door that she was standing as far away from him as she could without knocking over the stand of cue sticks behind her. It was not an inviting pose and the whole house was likely to hear her slap him if he dared to touch her so intimately. Last night she might've accepted his kisses, but not today.

'What's wrong, Clara?' Hugh ventured in a low voice, keeping an ear out for any footsteps in the hallway. This wasn't a particularly clever hiding place but in his eagerness to be alone with her it had seemed like the best choice.

'What makes you think there's anything wrong?' Clara crossed her arms over her chest, her stance less welcoming than it had been in the entry hall.

'After yesterday, I thought you'd enjoy this kind of game.'

'Then you guessed wrong.' She trilled her fingers on her bare upper arm, her fingertips brushing the smooth creaminess he wished he could caress.

'What happened since we parted last night?

You weren't this sharp or callous with me yesterday.'

His directness made her lips form an enticing *O* of shock before she regained her voice. 'I heard a very enthralling story at breakfast, one that involves you and a certain widow in London. It appears you have a fondness for intimate friendships with widows.'

'What do you mean?' He didn't defend himself for there was no defence against the truth. He thought she'd already heard that story, but apparently she hadn't. However, if she were bold enough to throw his past relationship in his face, one that had nothing to do with her, then he would see how much bolder she was in pursuing this line of discussion.

'Lady Frances. I understand she and you were…' She stopped, too embarrassed to say the word. She didn't need to say it because he did.

'Lovers. Yes, we were.' She wanted the truth and he would give it to her and prove that he was still the honest man she once believed in despite his questionable past.

Clara struggled to keep her jaw from dropping at his blunt answer. She hadn't expected him to so readily admit his sins and yet he'd confessed with all the frankness of a grocer telling her the price of apples. 'I don't know whether to forgive you for your honesty or lecture you about your vices.'

'My past vices,' he corrected, his words much tighter than they'd been when he'd led her to this hiding place. 'And you needn't lecture me. My mother did enough of that when she was alive. Trust me, she was no more thrilled by my time in London than you are.'

'I don't blame her.' No doubt he'd hoped by coming here to do something more pleasurable than discuss his mistress while they'd hid. She was glad to disappoint him. 'Is your time with Lady Frances really over?'

'It is and it never should have happened, but things were different for me then, and like you she was free to make her own decisions.'

'I'm nothing like her.'

'No, you're not.'

'Are you disappointed?'

'Not at all.'

This took the angry wind out of her sails, but it didn't settle the anxiety that had forced her to speak. 'Lord Westbook said you weren't willing to marry her.'

'Did he?' He ground his jaw, his shoulders and neck stiff, so unlike the Hugh who'd charmed her into almost making her forget herself in front of everyone last night.

'He did.' She never would have believed that she would be quoting Lord Westbook of all people. She couldn't stand the pompous man and yet she'd been all too willing to listen and believe him this morning, except what he'd said was true, at least the part about Lady Frances being Hugh's mistress. The rest she still wondered about.

'Then allow me to tell you what he doesn't know. A few months into our relationship, I offered to make Lady Frances an honest woman. She turned me down. My title was grand enough for her, but not my income. It was the beginning of the end of our rather weak relationship.'

His unwillingness to mince words forced Clara back into silence. She should be glad that someone who'd been all too willing to marry a woman for money had discovered what it was like to be rejected because he didn't have enough of it, but she wasn't. Instead she was left once again to try to reconcile the things he told her with what she knew of him and decide whether to believe his words or his actions. Deep down, she should trust her instincts and not the whisperings of a well-known gossip monger like Lord Westbook or the doubt he'd tried to plant in her, but her instincts had been wrong about Hugh before. If she chose to believe he was a scoundrel, then turning away from Hugh would be easier. Admitting he wasn't meant admitting to so many other things that terrified her, including how afraid she was of being wronged and humiliated again and how much the longing in Hugh's eyes matched the one in her heart.

Every bit of common sense and the awful lesson she'd learned from her previous experience with him screamed against this insanity, but still she could not dismiss it. All his supposed honesty could be nothing more than a ruse to gain her trust and then deceive her again. With troubles still facing Everburgh, he could be pursuing her simply because of her wealth, or because he did genuinely care for her. She didn't know which and she was tired of this ambiguity. 'What is it you want from me, Hugh?'

'The faith you showed in me yesterday and last night.'

'Why?'

'Because if you can believe in me again, then the man I used to be and wish to be again is not lost.'

Clara fingered the cold, smooth top of a cue ball sitting in a tray beside her, unsure how to respond. He was giving her opinion of him far more importance than it merited. 'Surely there are other people who can better offer you what you seek.'

'None with heartfelt honesty like yours. You don't play games, Clara, or ever leave me in doubt about your true feelings.'

'Or perhaps it's simply because I'm here and convenient, a single mistake from your past you can easily remedy on your way home in order to clear your conscience.'

'Is that all you think you are to me?'

'I don't know what I am to you. I never have.' He'd given her so many reasons for why he'd done the things he'd done, but he'd never admitted to loving her. She wanted this more than any apology or excuse, but her pride wouldn't allow her to ask for it. She'd stood in front of him, waiting for him to ask her to be his wife, and instead he'd told her the honour would go to another. She wasn't about stand here and demand his heart and listen to him give her a thousand reasons why it couldn't be hers, all of them very noble. She wasn't so hard up for love as to do this to herself.

'You're so much more than you realise.' He stepped up to her, towering over her in the semi-darkness of the small space. She stared at him, the shadows beneath his eyes darkening his brow while the light from beneath the door highlighted the angle of his chin. Beneath the musty smell of old equipment and dust, she caught the faint scent of his shaving soap and the earthier smell of horse and sweat from his morning ride. It was an enticing scent that took her back to Winsome and the many days spent with him and Adam running through the garden, before their time under the mistletoe had ruined the charm of those memories. She'd come here to set the past aside and claim a new future, and so had he, yet here they were together with everything that had passed between them still hanging in the air like the fine dust they'd disturbed.

She didn't know how to settle it, especially the quiet part of her that remembered what it was like to love him, to experience hope and possibility in his arms. If she reached out her hand and laid it on the side of his face, she could touch it all again, not the misery but the happiness, but fear kept her hands firmly at her sides. His sudden care for her might be nothing more than his old regard for her family and Adam and have little to do with the true preferences of his heart. Except the way he looked at her was more than admiration for her family, but the desire of a man to cross the darkness and take her in his arms.

Clara took a step closer to Hugh, then stopped, unwilling to give way completely to the temptation urging them closer together. If he made the first move and crossed the short distance that seemed like miles, then she would take a chance and go against every logical thought she had about him and follow him, but he must be the one to make his intentions clear in his touch, to tell her in his kiss that he truly meant everything he said to her, that it wasn't simply the heat of the moment like it had been before and when the clouds of infatuation cleared he would walk away from her again. She held her breath as she waited for him to lean down and press his lips to hers, to reveal the truth of his intentions in his kiss. He moved slowly, closing his eyes as she closed hers, his mouth so close she could almost taste him.

Suddenly, light spilled into the room, making Clara and Hugh flinch and raise their hands to cover their eyes. They stepped back from one another, the moment lost.

'It looks like I've found two more.' Lord Stanhope stood with the door open, smiling in triumph at them. 'At this rate the game will be over long before the gong rings.'

Clara stumbled past him and into the hallway, her heart pounding as she blinked against the shock of the light. Near misses with Hugh were quickly becoming the rule instead of the exception and if Lord Stanhope had been a moment later, he would have had quite a story for the breakfast table. There'd been nothing sordid about the encounter, no furtive clawing at one another or adjusting of clothes but there was no mistaking that Lord Stanhope's arrival had interrupted something. It wouldn't take much for him to guess what and for the story to be all over the house by the time the ball started, assuming he wasn't a discreet man. She didn't know enough about him to say if he was discreet or not. Clara pressed her hand to her chest, trying to work out the tightness sitting there. She should have known better than to have tempted Hugh and fate and yet once again she'd ignored her better senses and thrown off caution, to her detriment. It seemed like she would never learn.

She slowly turned to face Hugh and Lord Stanhope, smoothing the front of her dress with her hands while she composed herself. She tried to appear as if nothing untoward had been taking place in the cupboard, but for all her fear at their near miss, there was regret, too. If she and Hugh had kissed, her lingering questions about him might have been answered. Instead, what remained was confusion and the possibility for more humiliation.

'Lord Stanhope,' Hugh greeted their finder with little enthusiasm, as troubled by the interruption as her.

'Lord Delamare. It's been a while, but you appear well, certainly better than the last time I saw you. Where was it? Ah, yes, I remember.' He snapped his fingers. 'The field outside London. You'd winged Lord Cecil and secured your honour. What was it he'd called you?'

'I don't recall.' Hugh glanced back and forth between Clara and Lord Stanhope, clearly not appreciating this reminiscence so close on the heels of the one he'd been forced to endure about Lady Frances.

'I wish I could be so cavalier about a duel.' Lord Stanhope chuckled. 'Not that I've ever fought one.'

'Shall I call you out for finding us?'

Lord Stanhope held up his hands up in mock defence. 'I'm only doing my hostess's bidding.'

'And we can't fault him for that, can we, Lord Delamare?' Clara added, drawing his attention away from Hugh and the discomfort marring the moment. 'We surrender and wish you luck with the rest of your search.'

'Thank you, Lady Kingston, yours is the most gracious concession I've encountered this morning.' Lord Stanhope took her hand and raised it to his lips, his eyes never leaving hers and making her swallow hard. He was a potent reminder of everything that might be waiting for her if she stopped looking back and chose instead to move forward.

'I'm happy to be such a good sportsman.' Clara glanced over his shoulder to see Hugh watching them, his eyes clouded with irritation.

He's jealous. Clara inwardly smiled in triumphant delight, for she wanted him to see that she wasn't a simple girl new to love who could be wooed away from her better sense by a gentleman capable of overawing her, but a mature woman whose good opinion he must work to secure. She also wanted him to know that he was not the only one capable of claiming her attention.

Following the line of her gaze, Lord Stanhope let go of her and turned to Hugh, his smile dimming to a more humble grin. 'Off you both go to the dining room. Lady Tillman instructed me to tell all the people I find that the noon repast is served. It seems we are to be treated to a theatrical performance by the children this afternoon.'

With a bow, Lord Stanhope turned and wandered off down the hall in search of more guests.

'Shall we go to lunch?' Clara asked when

they were alone again, not sure what else to say.

'You go. I have some business to attend to before this afternoon.'

She didn't try to convince him to accompany her. They needed time apart after the confines of cupboard and everything they'd discussed, especially with them swinging from being at each other's throats to almost venturing into a place she wasn't certain either of them was ready to travel.

She wandered down the hall towards the dining room, glad there wasn't anyone else about. It allowed her to compose herself before she faced the others. For the second time in less than a day she'd been tempted by Hugh and almost too weak to resist. She hoped he didn't knock on her bedroom door tonight for she was beginning to doubt her ability to send him away. A little space to breathe was a very necessary thing.

Hugh watched Clara go, her yellow dress swaying about her legs and brushing her hips as she walked. His gaze remained fixed on her until she turned a corner and was out of sight, and then the regret rushed in. In an effort to be close to her, to answer the questions she'd asked him and the temptation he'd seen in her eyes, he'd nearly kissed her. In doing so, he'd almost opened her up to more gossip.

Except it wasn't just his mistakes that ate at him as he made his way to the study to try to distract himself with correspondence, but Lord Stanhope. He knew little about Lord Stanhope despite having seen him on more than one occasion at the theatre or his club, but there was no missing his obvious interest in Clara. Nor had Hugh failed to notice how willing she'd been to return his smiles, reminding Hugh again of the challenges he faced where it came to her. She had every right to show interest in a man who hadn't already wronged her and didn't bear a rake's reputation, at least not one he was aware of. If Hugh were willing to tolerate Lord Westbook for more than a second or two, he might sit down with the man and discover what he knew about Lord Stanhope, but he could imagine how that would set tongues wagging about Hugh sizing up the competition.

The more the image of Lord Stanhope bowing over Clara's hand and her basking in his attention tortured him, the more the patience he'd vowed to employ with her last night began to desert him. He'd lost her quickly once before when, after leaving Stonedown, she'd met Lord Kingston and then married him in a matter of months. If Hugh left her at the end of the party without a clear understanding of his future intentions, he might lose her again. When she'd stepped close to him in the closet, as eager for his touch as she'd been last night, he'd realised there was still hope for them to be together. Like all his opportunities to save Everburgh he must seize it. He might have lost his way for a while, but he wasn't a man to give up and he would not give up on a chance with Clara. It would mean risking his heart, but if it meant capturing hers and having her stand beside him in the struggles facing him, to remember what it was like to enjoy life the way he had last night and during the hunt yesterday, then it was worth the risk.

Chapter Eight

Dark clouds moved in to cover the blue sky in the hours after lunch, casting Stonedown deep into early winter darkness. Footmen lit the candles and chandeliers in the hallways and common rooms to drive back the encroaching gloom. Everyone was gathered in the sitting room to enjoy the children's theatrical performance. At the far end, a small stage had been erected and thick curtains hung on ropes draped either side of the boards.

Clara entered the impromptu theatre late, having spent the time after lunch in her bedroom enjoying the solitude and the chance to think uninterrupted about what had happened between her and Hugh in the closet. His past with Lady Frances was what she should focus on and how it was another in a long line of reasons why she should have nothing more to do with Hugh, except the incident didn't trouble her as much as she thought it would. While she hadn't liked finding out about his relationship with Lady Frances, he'd been honest with her instead of trying to hide behind lies or excuses. He didn't pretend, like everyone had when Lady Pariston had called attention to it, that such things didn't happen between men and women.

It was what had nearly happened before Lord Stanhope had stumbled in on them that troubled Clara far more than Hugh's previous dalliance. For the second time in as many days she'd almost kissed him. The man she'd vowed to be nothing more than friends with had almost become…what? She didn't know. She refused to be like Lady Frances and yet she'd almost fallen into Hugh's arms the moment he'd barcly reached out to her. It shocked and scared her how willing she'd been to do so. She shouldn't want him or have him mean anything more to her than a regrettable part of her past and perhaps as a future acquaintance, yet every time they were alone together they kept inching towards a line she'd never wanted drawn in the first place.

She longed to call it foolish weakness, but it was a great deal more. When he spoke of his troubles it was as if she was hearing herself speak. When he admitted his failings and weaknesses she could see her own and how the grief that had changed her had done the same to him. Outwardly, they seemed so different in how they had dealt with hardship, but inside they were very much alike and she could speak with him about it all because he understood. Even in the moments when she doubted his integrity, he offered her every reason why she shouldn't, undercutting all of her arguments against him and every advice about judging a man by his actions that her mother had ever given her. There was more to what he told her about his past than false words, but truth, reason, honour and grief. Then when he looked at her, as he had in the closet, it was as if she was the most precious thing in the world.

Her feelings about Hugh continued to baffle her, especially the closer she drew to the sitting room. She had no idea how she would greet Hugh or how to behave. It was wrong, but the more time she spent with him the harder it was to ignore logic and not listen to her heart. In his way, he was trying to help her put the pieces of it back together and she couldn't help but yearn for him.

Thankfully, Hugh wasn't in the sitting room and Clara let out a small sigh of relief. She took one of the empty chairs near the door, unnoticed by all the other guests who were enthralled with talk of their children and the upcoming joy of watching their little ones perform. The one good thing about worrying over Hugh was that it had distracted her from thinking about the play and her lack of a little player to watch. In the semi-shadows of the back of the room, the old pain rushed back to her, especially with the parents sitting in delight at the front where they deserved to be. As a marchioness, Clara might take precedence over all these people, but she would gladly trade that privilege to be sitting at the front row and waiting for a child of her own to step on to the boards. She turned her wedding band around on her finger, tired of waiting and mourning. At times this week when she'd been with Hugh, her losses hadn't hurt so much because he understood what it was like to lose one's future and dreams. With Hugh beside her she'd had someone to talk to whose care and concern gave her hope. Without him here, it was difficult to keep the sadness at bay.

Her private moment was short-lived as Lord Stanhope entered the room. He stopped on the threshold, taking in the guests and the available seats before spying the empty one beside her. Flashing a wide smile, he made directly for her. She should be flattered that he wished to sit with her, but something in the way he regarded her that didn't quite liven his eyes, so unlike Hugh with his natural admiration, made her wish he would chose a different seat. He appeared to be a pleasant enough man, but there was an exaggerated aspect to his pleasantness that was difficult for Clara to put into words or to dismiss.

'Good afternoon, Lady Kingston. May I?' He pointed to the chair.

Clara was about to tell him to sit when Hugh came up behind Lord Stanhope, stepped around him and took the empty seat. 'Excuse me, Lord Stanhope, but this is my place.'

Clara gaped at Hugh while Lord Stanhope's charming smile went stiff about the sides. If Clara was not mistaken, distaste for Hugh flashed through his eyes before he covered it with a bow of defeat. 'Of course, Lord Delamare.'

Lord Stanhope made for the opposite side of the room and the empty chair beside Lord Worth.

'Rather forward of you, don't you think?' Clara asked, more charmed than annoyed by the little tiff over who had the right to sit beside her. It was the first time in her life that two men had vied for her attention and, far from being annoyed with Hugh's heavy-handed deciding of the matter, she was flattered.

'Not at all. I outrank him.' Hugh tilted up his head in mock arrogance. 'Can't have these lower men thinking too much of themselves, now, can we?'

'No, not at all.' Clara stifled a giggle. 'To think that a mere…um… What is he?'

'The Second Baron Stanhope.'

'That a baron, and only a second one at that, can sit next to a marchioness is outrageous.'

'If I'd allowed his impertinence to stand,

who knows what might have happened. Viscounts could challenge earls and then there would be no end to the chaos in line before dinner.'

This time Clara didn't hold back her laughter, glad to enjoy herself and their jokes instead of enduring the tension of her accusations and his defence and her loss. She slid a sideways glance at Hugh, taking in the tight cut of his breeches against his firm thighs, the close fit of his waistcoat about his trim middle and the strength of him that called to her more than she cared to admit. It could happen between her and Hugh if she wanted it to, as Anne and Lady Pariston had suggested. All she need do was slip down the dark hall tonight to his room, but she wouldn't. It was an entanglement some women could indulge in without risk to their hearts, but not her. She wanted a man's whole life, not simply the sordid pieces hidden by the dark and not spoken of in polite society. If he could give her this, then she would be his, but he had to offer it, to make it clear to her and everyone that this time his affection for her was real and his promises to her would be kept.

'What play do you think we will be treated to today?' Hugh asked, his breath brushing the side of her cheek and making the desire swirling inside her to go to his room tonight even stronger.

'I don't know, but I'm sure it will be a riveting production,' Clara whispered, fighting to control this silly temptation. Thankfully, the performance began and Clara clapped with the rest of the audience as the youngest of the children took to the stage amidst a great deal of oohs and ahhs from the parents.

The sons and daughters of the guests, the littlest being about four years old and the oldest not quite out of the nursery performed a Christmas play about the Lord of Misrule and some of the antics he got up to during a Christmas house party.

Clara watched the performers, but it was difficult to concentrate on even the scenes with her niece and nephew with Hugh sitting so close. More than once, his thigh brushed the skirt of her dress when he moved, making the soft fabric caress her bare skin beneath.

'They're fun to watch, aren't they?' Hugh asked when James and another boy, both of them dressed as knights, began a mock battle on stage.

'Yes, they are,' Clara answered in a weak voice, trying to retain her smile as the all-too-familiar pain began to well inside her. Despite the joy of watching little James, the presence of Hugh and the jokes they'd shared before the start of the performance, she couldn't hold back the sadness. If things had been different, Clara would be in the front of the room beside Adam and Anne, clapping enthusiastically for a well-delivered line and beaming with the same pride that decorated the few faces she could see from where she sat.

The longer the performance went, the more thoughts of Hugh beside her faded, replaced by an emptiness that made her chest ache until she could no longer sit still. Without making her excuses to Hugh, she rose and fled the room, doing all she could to not draw attention to herself. She didn't wish to dull anyone else's enthusiasm for they had the right to enjoy their children's performance without her pain ruining it.

In the shadows of the hallway where the voices of the little mites were muted by the distance, Clara stopped. Wrapping her hands about her waist, she took a few deep breaths, doing her best to calm herself and regain control. It was one thing to cry in her room alone and quite another to do it where anyone might happen upon her. It also angered her. She thought she'd got over these fits of melancholy ages ago, but she hadn't. They weren't as frequent as they used to be, but they still hurt and she was helpless to do anything but endure them until they passed. They were something she did not speak about, not even to Anne, not wanting to be pitied. There was no one else to talk to because everyone else expected her to have moved past it, to forget. She wished it was so easy to forget, but it wasn't.

'Are you all right, Clara?' Hugh asked, his voice soothing and comforting in the dim light of the hall.

Clara turned to face him, glad it was he and not someone else who'd stumbled on her. The closer he came, the more she wanted to throw herself in his arms and wet the wool of his coat with her tears. She wanted him to hold her and tell her that she wasn't alone in her grief and that all was well and that, in time, everything would be all right, but she didn't move. She longed to be brave as she always was in front of everyone, but she couldn't lie to him either. She was tired of enduring the isolating grief that swathed her in moments like this, helpless to do more than let it wash over her until it passed. Perhaps if she gave it words it might release its hold on her and she could once again enjoy such simple delights as children performing at Christmas without the threat of tears.

'Sometimes it's difficult to see what others have and be reminded that it's not a joy I share. I don't wish them ill or that they go without like I do, but it hurts to not have a little one of my own.'

'Some day you will applaud as enthusiastically for your child delivering their stilted lines as much as Adam and Anne,' Hugh assured her in a gentle voice, coming to stand in front of her.

'I want to believe that, but it's so difficult.' During her marriage, Clara had consulted the midwife who, finding nothing wrong with her, had said it must be Alfred. He'd suffered from an awful bout of scarlet fever as a child and the midwife had heard stories of men fathering no more children after such illnesses. Given that he and his first wife had not been blessed, this had seemed right, but Clara had always held out hope that time might have proven the old woman wrong, but there hadn't been enough of it. 'I wish with all my heart that I had something more than a title and a widow's portion to remind me of my former life.' The one that had ended too soon, the memories of which were fading more and more every day.

'You will find love again and have a child some day.'

In the background, the high voices of the children delivering their lines rang out in the room along with the occasional chuckles and ahhs of their parents.

'That's what everyone says.' She turned away from him and stared up at the portrait of some past Lady Tillman in her heavy velvet dress and wide, ruffled-lace collar. Shc stood with her hand on the shoulder of her son, both of them looking out from the canvas in confidence. 'But it's difficult to believe sometimes. What if I never meet anyone else?'

'You will, I promise you.' He came up behind her and laid his hands comfortingly on her shoulders, their weight stronger than the melancholy draping her. 'Don't give up, Clara.'

His low voice in her ear was as soothing as it was warm against her skin. Six years ago, when she'd been hurting, Alfred had come to her and helped her. Now she was hurting in a different way and here was Hugh doing the same. She leaned into him, his comfort meaning more to her than anyone else's because he'd experienced this, too. His spouse and every dream he'd had of a child with her had been stolen from him, leaving him, like Clara, to find his way to whatever the future held for him.

'Sometimes I find it hard not to give up.'

'We've both tried giving up before, you with Winsome, me in London and it didn't help either of us.' He tightened his arms round her, his chin close to her temple as he held her and spoke. 'If we give up, then we will lose and we'll really have nothing. I don't want to have nothing. That's a pain I can't live with, more than mourning or anything. It's why I'm here, to try to make things better.'

She closed her eyes, the resolution in his words giving her strength. With his firm arms around her she could believe that some day it would be her in a portrait with her children or her clapping for her child's performance. Behind her his chest rose and fell with each of his long breaths, his arms tight against her chest. She raised her hands to rest them on the soft wool of his coat, revelling in the safety and contentment of his embrace. He pressed a kiss to her temple, his tenderness making her sigh. In his embrace there was more than comfort or need, but the answer to the questions she'd asked in the cupboard and the truth she'd sought all last night and most of today. She opened her eyes and looked up at the copper flecks in his brown eyes as he watched her. He hadn't sought her out because of money or boredom, but because he truly did care for her as much as she did him and it would all be different this time.

She could have stood within the security of his arms for hours, but applause thundered out of the sitting room accompanied by shouts of 'Bravo'.

'I think the performance is over.' Clara reluctantly straightened and Hugh let go of her. Despite what had happened between them, they stood where anyone leaving the sitting room could see them. 'James and Lillie will expect me to be there to congratulate them.'

'Then let's not disappoint them.'

Clara walked beside Hugh back into the sitting room, the quiet between them more comfortable than words. The awkwardness of the cupboard, of their first dinner and all the near misses vanished like the smoke from the candles, as did Clara's doubts about him. She'd come downstairs this morning eager for clarity about Hugh and in his arms in the hallway she'd found it. He wasn't the schemer who would break her heart, but a man she could reveal her fears and weaknesses to without worrying that he would laugh or make her regret being so open.

They entered the sitting room and were met by the sight of proud parents hugging their little players, fathers holding up their sons and mothers cuddling their daughters. While they watched the parents congratulate their children, no one, not even Lord Westbook or Lady Fulton, noticed them in back so far from the candle footlights. In the semi-darkness, Hugh stretched out his hand to touch hers. Clara didn't pull away but turned her hand to accept his caresses. In his touch was the promise that their turn to be this happy and content with children and families and estates would come, too. Some day, she would return to Stonedown filled with the love of a husband and the joy of children. She had no idea when it might happen, but under the influence of Hugh's encouragement and the pressure of his touch she believed that she was a little closer to claiming it. She would not give up or allow grief and isolation to keep her from gaining the things she craved. She would strive on, as Hugh urged, and succeed.

Chapter Nine

Clara entered the Holyfield ballroom beside Anne, pausing a moment on the threshold to search for Hugh. Among the dresses that had arrived from Winsome had been a light pink one with a flowing silk skirt and a bodice of rich velvet embroidered with silver thread that sparkled when she walked like the sapphires around her neck. The jewels had been her mother's and in the family for three generations, but she wore them tonight as if they were hers and no one else's. A number of people on both the dance floor and the crowd around it turned to take her in, eyes wide with amazement or with smiles of approval. However, it wasn't for them that she'd chosen this dress and necklace, but for Hugh.

After the play, convention had forced them

apart and the demands of preparing for tonight had left them without another chance to speak, but the unspoken promises that had passed between them in the hallway, and again when he'd taken her hand, had been enough to carry her through the rest of the day. All the doubt that Lord Westbook and others had tried to sow in her, and all the second guessing she'd done since the beginning of the party, were over. Whoever Hugh had been in London, he was no longer that man, he never had been, but like her he'd been lost and hurting. Except when they were together the pain could not touch them. She'd leaned in to him today without thinking and he'd offered her the support of his body and his experiences to comfort and hold her. She couldn't throw that away out of fear of what people might think or out of her own worries that the past might repeat itself. Neither of those things was important any more. Hugh had reminded her that what had happened before was gone and only the present and the future mattered, and she wanted him to be a part of both and for that life to begin tonight. She could love him again and she felt certain that his heart was hers already.

The shifting forward of the receiving line forced Clara to stop searching the room and greet Lord and Lady Elmswood, the owners of Holyfield. The arrival of guests from Stonedown had been slowed by the snow that had begun to fall at sunset and the many carriages needed to convey everyone to the ball. Thankfully, the snow had not come down hard enough to block the roads and prevent anyone from reaching this Tudor wood and plaster house with the magnificent wood-beamed great room. The numerous rafters were decorated with garlands of evergreens that infused the air with the scent of pine. Clara did her best to concentrate on Lady Elmswood while they spoke, careful not to keep looking about in search of Hugh. She didn't know which carriage he'd ridden in or if he was here already or waiting to arrive. He might be in the card room, watching the play or enjoying refreshment from the Elmwoods' generous outlay.

No, if he was here, he would be waiting for me.

Clara flexed her hand where a few hours before Hugh had touched his bare skin to hers. The impression of it had lingered long after the parents leaving the sitting room had forced them apart. She wanted to see him again, to dance and be with him and experience once more the optimism and hope of his presence. When he was near, she felt as if anything was possible and it was a feeling she was loath to lose.

'Searching for someone?' Anne nudged Clara with her elbow as they made their way along the edge of the dance floor after leaving Lady Elmswood.

'Perhaps I am?' Clara answered in a singsong voice, not irritated by Anne's continued interest in Clara and Hugh. Soon everyone would be aware of it and it didn't matter. She didn't care what they thought of her or Hugh or what they said about them being together. From here on out, no one's opinion but her own would guide her or hold so much importance.

'I'm glad to hear it.' Anne snapped open her fan and waved in front of her face, making the ruby earrings dangling from her small ears swing with the slight breeze. 'I wouldn't mind if you two renewed your former friendship.'

'Is friendship all you're interested in seeing

between us?' Clara enjoyed torturing Anne as Anne had enjoyed doing it with her.

Except Anne suddenly turned serious. 'I want to see you well settled again, Clara, and despite what happened before, I do believe that Lord Delaware could make you happy if you gave him a chance.'

Clara clasped her fan in front of her, tempted to tell Anne that the chance had already been taken, but she didn't. This was no place to explain to her that she had changed her mind or why. She wasn't sure she could explain it in a manner that anyone, even Anne, could understand. She barely understood it herself.

'You needn't make any decisions yet,' Anne assured, pointing over Clara's shoulder. 'For look who's coming to join us.'

Clara's heart began to race and she stood up straight, careful to maintain the grace and confidence that she'd carried with her into Holyfield. Slowly she turned around, waiting for the moment when Hugh saw her and she could bask in his attention.

Lord Stanhope approached her with the stealth of a tiger. All Clara's excitement vanished at the sight of him and she struggled to maintain her smile and her manners. 'Lady Kingston, I'm so glad you've arrived for I haven't forgotten your promise.'

'My promise?' She could barely remember having spoken to the man today much less making him any promises. It was Hugh who had commanded her attention when present and who continued to do so even while they were apart.

'To give me your first dance.'

'Oh, yes.' She had promised this and with Hugh having yet to arrive, she had no choice but to place her hand in Lord Stanhope's and allow him to lead her out on to the dance floor.

While they walked, there was no fluttering in her chest like there was whenever she touched Hugh. She marvelled at this for Lord Stanhope was very handsome with manners to charm the teeth out of a snake. The two of them walking together garnered a number of looks. They weren't the looks of amazed curiosity that had startled so many at the Holyfield ball six years ago when people must have wondered what it was that the Marquess of Delamare had seen in the quiet and shy Exton girl, but genuine awe at a bejewelled marchioness being escorted by a handsome lord to her rightful place on the dance floor. Clara should have revelled in the moment, but everyone's admiration paled against her desire to be beside Hugh.

The musicians struck the first notes and she and Lord Stanhope began the dance, hands touching and raised in the air between to make the required turns.

'You are quite stunning tonight,' Lord Stanhope complimented, this one, like all his others, too exuberant and almost studied for Clara to take seriously.

'Thank you, but as we have not met before, how do you know I'm not this stunning every night?' Clara enjoyed this flirting and the power she felt in it—it was a prelude to everything she hoped to enjoy with Hugh.

'I'm sure you are this stunning every night, as I'm certain to discover during the rest of my time at Stonedown.'

He was very much overestimating how much time the two of them would spend together if he thought so.

'What brings you to Stonedown, Lord Stanhope?' Clara searched the people watching them, but still did not see Hugh. She wondered if he'd decided at the last minute not to come. No, he had to be here, to want to see and be with her as much as she longed to be with him. The snow must have delayed his arrival. All would be well, just like he'd promised. She was certain of it.

'The promise of charming company is the reason I'm here.' Lord Stanhope made the turn around her this time, his eyes never leaving hers, their intensity almost laughable if it weren't for the seriousness of his look. 'What other reason could there be?'

'There must be plenty of charming company in London.' Most of whom would enjoy his constant flattery and charm more than her.

'I find the company of the country far more lively and refreshing than what's available in town. Unless you decide to venture there next spring?'

'I have not decided.' She had no desire to make him any more promises.

He raised her hand again and held it while she made a turn. As she came around him, facing out to the audience, she finally spied Hugh across the room standing with Sir Nathaniel and Adam. A small muscle along the side of his jaw twitched while he watched Lord Stanhope place his arm around her to promenade. She didn't feel Lord Stanhope's touch, but longed instead to be in Hugh's arms.

She endured many more of these turns and promenades, catching Hugh's eye during each one. It took all her strength to remain beside Lord Stanhope and not dart off to join Hugh, for the dance lasted much longer than she remembered. During it all, she was polite and cordial as expected of a woman of her rank, but her heart was across the room with Hugh.

Finally, the musicians brought the piece to an end and Lord Stanhope offered her the most gallant of bows before escorting her off the dance floor. Once they were back in the crowd, he turned to her as if he was about to ask for another dance when Hugh appeared beside him.

'Lady Kingston.' Hugh held out his hand for her to take, ignoring Lord Stanhope and making clear to him, and Clara, that he was not to expect any more dances for Hugh would be her partner.

She pressed her gloved palm to his and he

closed his fingers over hers, claiming her as she wished to be claimed.

At the far end of the room, the musicians began the slow melody of a waltz. A murmur of excitement raced through the room with everyone amazed that Lady Elmswood would sanction such a dubious dance. It didn't stop them from choosing their partners and hurrying out to the dance floor to delight in this near-scandalous endeavour.

'Shall we?' Hugh asked, his voice as husky as if he were leading her into his bedroom.

'Yes, please.' She was eager for him to place his hand at her waist and to clasp his other around hers. As much as she needed a good country dance with a great deal of sashaying to help quell the energy building inside her at being this close to Hugh, she was glad for the intimacy of the waltz. She could be alone with him in this small way, free to speak and enjoy the strong lines of his face, his deep voice and pleasant smile without censure.

He led her to the centre of the dance floor and turned her to face him, laying his strong hand on her waist and taking her hand with the other. Then he stepped close, towering over her with his wide shoulders and solid chest, his heady cologne mixing with the pine fragrance filling the room. She took a deep breath as much to savour the nearness of him as to steady herself. Then he set them both into motion in time to the slow melody. Her skirt whispered against his legs with each sure step and his fingers tightened against her middle as he led her in the dance. Clara held tight to his shoulder, wishing she could stretch out her fingers and caress the smooth skin of his neck. Once in a while, his thigh brushed against hers, the tease of it almost making her knees buckle, but he held her in the sturdy circle of his arms and she didn't falter. With his gaze riveted to hers, the ballroom and everyone in it seemed to fade away until it was just the two of them and the music. She surrendered to his lead, allowing him to sweep her along and deeper in to him.

'You look stunning tonight, Clara.' Hugh's compliment was unstudied in a way that Lord Stanhope's had not been. It'd been too long since she'd received such sincere praise, especially from someone who mattered.

'Thank you.'

'What were you and Lord Stanhope discussing?'

'London and whether I will venture there for the Season.'

'And will you?'

She tilted her head to gaze up at him through her eyelashes. 'Is there a reason for me to go there beyond trying to catch a napping lord?'

'I will be there.' He pulled her a touch closer, his coat brushing her waist when they moved.

She shifted her hand on his shoulder a bit closer to his neck and allowed one finger to brush his skin. 'Then that is a good reason for me to go.'

He turned his head enough to make his chin graze the back of her hand, his lips so close to her skin, he could almost kiss her. Her entire body tingled with anticipation, but they couldn't be so intimate, not here in front of everyone. Someone might be watching, but if they were Clara didn't notice. She could only see Hugh and all the possibility for their future in his eyes.

At the end of the room, the musicians brought the dance to a close. Hugh stopped, but didn't let go of her until holding on made them stand out and he at last removed his hand from her back, but not his hold on her hand. He raised it to his lips as he bowed to her, viewing her from beneath his brow with a look to take her breath away. 'I think we have a spectacular new year to look forward to.'

'I think we do.'

With the couples around them shifting off the floor and quickly being replaced by new dancers, Hugh tucked her arm into the crook of his elbow and escorted her into the crowd. They didn't stop, but continued towards the back of the room and to a hallway leading off the ballroom. It was quiet here and far from the glare of the chandeliers illuminating the beam-ceilinged great room. Paintings of horses and dogs sprinting across the landscape dotted the hallway along with a generous sprig of mistletoe that hung from the small chandelier in the centre. Hugh guided her beneath the sprig and together they stared up at the single berry clinging to the stem. The kiss it conferred on them could be theirs if Hugh leaned forward and touched his lips to hers. Clara very much hoped that he would, defying the small voice in the back of her mind that said she shouldn't be standing here with him where anyone who wandered by would see them together. That voice was blotted out by the longing to be free and to not care. She was a widow and for all the heartache it'd foisted on her, Lady Pariston was right, it also gave her more leniency to do as she pleased in a way she never could have enjoyed as an unmarried woman. She would use it to be brave with Hugh and to not doubt herself or him or this Christmas. It would be the first of what was sure to be many happy ones to come.

'It seems a pity to leave it hanging there, all alone.' He flicked a glance up to the mistletoe and the single berry still clinging to its stem. 'To think of it being burned with the rest of the greenery when the Christmas season is over and never fulfilling its duty to those standing beneath it.'

Clara's heart began to race and she tilted her head back a touch to flash him an amused and inviting look, enjoying this rush of boldness. 'We can't have that, now can we?'

'Not at all.' He stepped forward and took Clara's hands, towering over her in strength, but with a tenderness to touch her heart. He leaned forward, his gaze never leaving hers until she closed her eyes, waiting for their lips to meet.

When they did, every part of her came alive. She inhaled his breath and the subtle scent of his sandalwood shaving soap made more potent by the sweat from their last dance. Raising her hands, she laid them on his shoulders, holding on tight to him to steady herself against the thrill making her tremble. She revelled in the press of his lips and the soft weight of her in his arms around her waist and his breath caressing his face. There were a hundred reasons why she shouldn't be here alone with his mouth claiming hers and his tongue drawing out hers to savour the taste of him, but none of them mattered. This was no mere groping or illicit stolen moment, but something more. It was there in the light way he held her, in the restraint in his lips and the promise she'd seen in his eyes before they'd kissed.

Hugh savoured the sweet taste of Clara as the lively notes of the musicians' stringed instruments accompanied by the steady murmur and laughter of voices carrying out of the ballroom swirled around them. When he'd stepped into the ballroom and seen her dancing with Lord Stanhope, smiling and laughing at the gentleman as if he were the most charming man in the room, every fear he'd had about losing her by holding back had seized him. Then he'd approached her and the widening of her smile that had made her beam like the mirrors reflecting the candlelight told him that he couldn't lose her for she was already his. All he need do was pick up where they had left off six years ago, before duty and responsibilities had forced him away from her. Those things might still be with him, but so was Clara, as free to be his as he was to be hers. With her by his side, he would strive to finally secure Everburgh and make it everything he and his family had wanted it to be, and to make her his Marchioness.

The tempting rise and fall of her chest against his made his pulse pound in his ears. Beneath the fine fabric of her dress he could feel the subtle boning of her stays and the curve of her hips below a small waist. With her firm body beneath his palms he longed for the freedom to be with her, the one denied to him six years ago and the one he would deny himself again until she could be truly and legally his.

He slid one hand up the curve of her waist and along the length of her bare arm above her glove to cup her cheek. She willingly fell deeper into his embrace and opened her lips to take in the gentle sweep of his tongue against hers. In the air between them, her rosewater perfume blotted out the fresh fragrances of the pines and evergreens heralding the approach of Christmas. All too soon the kiss was over and he leaned back, leaving his arms around her to steady himself against the rush of feeling making him want to clasp her to him again. He brushed a wisp off hair off of her cheek and tucked it behind her ear. Her skin was warm and soft against his palm and she looked up at him, her eyes sparkling like the jewels adorning her neck. 'I'll be sorry to see the party end.'

'Me, too, but there are still a few days left.'

And many more chances to speak and be with Clara, to slip into dark corners and enjoy more of her kisses and her touch until the Christmas house party ended and they parted for the remainder of winter. Spring and the opening of Parliament couldn't come soon enough. He wouldn't avoid London this year, but join Clara for the Season and make it her last as an unmarried widow. The end of the Christmas season would not be the end of things between them, but the beginning of many wonderful years to come and all of them spent with Clara.

Hugh bent down, ready to claim her mouth once more when an all-too-familiar female voice purred in disgust, making Hugh freeze.

'Hugh, it's good to see you haven't changed.'

Clara jumped back out of Hugh's embrace, her heart racing at the starling interruption. Hugh didn't move so fast, slowly lowering his arms and straightening as he stiffly turned to take in the woman watching them at the entrance to the hall.

She was a stunning blonde, much taller than Clara with a certain poise that whispered of a London polish. Her dress was of the newest fashion and cut far lower than Clara would have ever dared, revealing an enviable bust. She wore nothing more than a gold chain against her luminous skin and small white flowers in the elaborate curls of her hair.

She barely spared a glance for Clara, taking in nothing more than her large diamond and sapphire necklace which Clara was glad she'd worn. She almost felt gaudy in it beside this woman, but her inclination to cover it with her fan ended at the annoyed curl of the woman's lips. Whoever this woman was, she was not happy to see Hugh with Clara and this set Clara on edge.

'Who is she?' Clara whispered to Hugh.

'Lady Elizabeth Frances,' Hugh said through clenched teeth.

Clara's jaw dropped as low as Lady Fulton's and Lord Westbook's who'd stepped into the hall just in time to witness this scene, curse the busybodies. Both of their eyes widened in amazement before Lady Fulton narrowed hers with relish at what appeared to be the makings of a good tale, and a chance to best Clara.

'What are you doing here?' Hugh demanded of Lady Frances.

'I'm a guest of Lady Tillman's,' she answered before Clara could warn her that they were not alone. 'My cousin is acquainted with her and applied to her for invitation.'

Lady Frances glided towards Hugh like a boat on calm water, the wispy fabric of her skirt clinging a little too much to her slender legs. She came so close to him she crowded out Clara, who had no choice but to step aside or be struck by the woman's enviable bosom. Lord Westbook and Lady Fulton took the opportunity to shift closer, too, stopping Lord and Lady Missington when they passed and encouraging them to watch. Clara was too stunned by all of this to reprimand any of them for so blatantly intruding on what was clearly a private conversation. 'London can be so cold and lonely this time of year, especially for a young widow.'

Hugh didn't answer, staring down at her not with the hot look one might expect for so finely built a woman, but with a disdain Clara felt creeping up her spine. His silence encouraged the woman to carry on.

'Ever since I arrived this evening I've been searching for you.' Her words sucked what remained of Clara's cheer out of the hallway the way the flue did the smoke from a fireplace.

'Now you've found me. What do you want?' His brusque question at last wiped the simpering smile off the woman's face.

Clara wanted to know, too, fearing that this ball was about to turn from the most magical into one as heartbreaking as the holiday six years ago.

Lady Frances stepped back, the same disgust filling Hugh's eyes making her blue eyes hard. 'To tell you I'm carrying your child.'

Chapter Ten

'Impossible, I tell you, it's impossible. We haven't seen each other for six months,' Hugh railed, storming the length of Adam's bedroom at Stonedown. Adam stood across from Hugh, listening to him rant. His friend already knew what had happened in the hallway at the ball beneath the mistletoe. Hugh was beginning to curse that damned plant.

After Elizabeth's none-too-subtle announcement, Clara had bolted from Hugh as fast as if he'd come down with the plague. Hugh had left soon after, not about to stand there and discuss so delicate a topic in such a public place. He'd returned to Stonedown, glad to see that Anne and Adam had possessed the clarity of mind to remove Clara from Holyfield and that Adam was still willing to speak with him. Hugh needed to explain the situation to the one man he could trust to listen without too much judgement. He would not lose this friendship because of a lying woman. 'She doesn't even look pregnant. Did you think she looked pregnant?'

'With the current style of gown it's difficult to tell. All ladies look as if they are a few months gone. I made the mistake of asking Anne if she was expecting once when she showed me a new gown. The look she gave me could have burned bread.'

'I tell you, Lady Frances is lying.' At a moment like this he wished he hadn't given up drinking, but he need a clear head to handle this situation. One fogged up with spirits was how he'd landed himself in this mess.

'I've heard no rumours of her taking up with another man and let's be honest, Hugh, she wasn't exactly discreet with you.'

'Well, she's either lying about the child or she's become far more discreet. Either way, she obviously came here to make a spectacle out of herself and trap me in marriage. It makes her claim even more dubious.'

'I agree that her method of approaching you was poorly planned and I have heard some rumours about her in London, especially in regards to debts.'

'There are richer and more gullible men she could trap without resorting to tricks or theatrics.' Suddenly the joke about Clara approaching sleeping lords and startling them into jumping to the altar didn't seem so amusing any more. Nor was the look of horror that had crossed her face before she'd left him. The trust and affection he'd spent hours working to gain over these last few days had been wrecked in a matter of moments and by the one person he'd never expected to see in the country. Lady Elizabeth Frances wasn't the country type.

'There are richer men,' Adam concurred, 'but, for whatever reason, she's chosen you.'

'You must believe me; the child isn't mine.' He couldn't even remember the last time he and Elizabeth had been intimate before they'd parted.

Adam picked up a silver comb off the dresser and tapped it against his palm. 'If the child is yours, will you do right by it?'

Hugh took a deep breath as the chains of duty tightened around him and for the second time Clara would be the one to suffer because of it. By morning the entire countryside would know about what had happened at Holyfield and in a few days all their friends would learn of it by letter. He could practically hear the people in the adjoining rooms scribbling on the parchment in delight about this scandalous new tale. It was everything he hadn't wanted, every complication he'd sought to avoid when it came to Clara. When he'd decided to pursue her a second time it'd been with the intention of acting honourably and safeguarding her heart and her trust in him. In one quick moment, everything he'd achieved with her had been destroyed. Heaven knew what Hugh would face when he saw Elizabeth again for she was sure to press her suit as publicly here at Stonedown as she'd done at Holyfield. With all the people eavesdropping on them at Holyfield, there hadn't been time to speak privately to Elizabeth. Hopefully she'd returned to Stonedown as quickly as Clara for Hugh needed to resolve this with her as soon, and as discreetly, as possible. Until then, too much hung in the balance. 'I must find a way to make her confess the truth.'

'And if what she's saying is the truth?'

'I tell you it isn't.' Hugh brought his fist down hard on the top of the mantel, making the porcelain figures decorating it rattle. 'And I won't lose Clara again because of some lying woman.'

'After Lady Frances's display tonight, I don't think Clara would have you even if Lady Frances stood in the middle of Rotten Row and declared some other man the father.'

Hugh dug his fists into his hips and stared at a scuff on the floor, the truth in Adam's words as difficult to hear as what Elizabeth had said. He'd seen Clara's cheeks flush with embarrassment and horror after Elizabeth's announcement. Then he'd heard the gasp of shock from Lady Fulton and Lord Westbook. Hugh, without meaning to, had humiliated her in front of the worst two people possible. No, she wasn't likely to speak to him again. 'It's never been my intention to hurt her, but always things appear so far beyond my control.'

Before, there'd been the threat of an engagement to Lady Hermione to temper his excitement with Clara, but this impediment had come at him out of nowhere. Hugh rested his elbow on the mantel and pressed his fingers against his forehead. Like the last challenge to Everburgh, no matter how hard he worked to free himself from debt and lawsuits and marriages of convenience, they sought him out like a hound does a fox and this time they were succeeding in bringing him down. 'I can only ask a woman to forgive me so many times before she runs out of patience and understanding.'

'Her brother, too. I'm afraid I must ask you not to come to Winsome in the New Year.'

Hugh lowered his hand and flexed his fingers before bringing them to rest on the cool marble. 'I understand and I'm sorry, Adam.'

He truly was for the pain he'd caused his friend and Clara, and for all the mistakes he'd made that had led them to this moment. During the meagreness of his childhood, his visits to Winsome had always been a chance to forget the hardships and deprivation at home, to enjoy being a boy without worrying about food or bills or the darkness of the manor. He'd hoped to find there with his oldest friend that same comfort again and yet by his own mistakes he'd ruined his ability to enjoy that kind of peace ever again. It tore at him as much as having lost Clara for a second time.

'I'm not the one you should apologise to,' Adam suggested.

'I will speak with her.' He didn't know when or how, for she wasn't likely to see him again, much less allow him to say the words, none of which would make this awful situation any better or repair the damage Elizabeth's scene had caused to Clara's opinion of Hugh and to his future. Once more, he'd been on the verge of finding love with Clara and it was being torn away from him. It made him doubt ever having left London, swearing off drink and devoting himself anew to duty. The desire to ring for a footman and demand a bottle of brandy or wine made his palms itch, but he held back, unable to go back on his promise to himself. He'd vowed to see all his troubles through and make a better life for himself and it was a vow he would damn well keep, one way or another. He wouldn't lose his head and falter, but remain strong and dignified as expected of a marquess. He would not be like his grandfather.

'How could he do such a thing?' Clara stormed back and forth across Anne's bedroom at Stonedown Manor, going over for the hundredth time what had happened. She'd found Anne moments after leaving the hallway, Lady Frances's announcement ringing in her ears as if she'd stood too close to a church bell during matins. Worse than that had been the glee decorating Lady Fulton's face and the realisation that Clara was no different than she'd been six years ago, and now everyone knew it. It made fresh tears spring to her eyes. 'How could I have been foolish enough to fall for his tricks a second time?'

'I saw him with you. I don't think they were tricks, Clara, not this time or the last.'

'Then why am I here crying with you and not at Holyfield dancing with Hugh? I can't believe this is happening again.' She wiped her cheeks with the back of her hands, the pain and humiliation cutting so deep she could barely breathe. All her hopes and dreams for this week, and her desires to prove to everyone that she'd changed, were lying in ruins at Holyfield.

'Perhaps Lady Tillman will rescind Lord Delamare and Lady Frances's invitation and the two of them will leave and take this awful situation away with them,' Anne offered with more hope than Clara possessed.

'Lady Tillman isn't likely to send anyone off in this weather. You saw how much harder the snow was coming down on our way home. By tomorrow morning the roads will be difficult to pass.' Clara wished the snow had come a few days sooner and stopped Lady Frances from arriving at all. However, all it would have done was postpone the inevitable, perhaps after Clara and Hugh had given more to each other than a kiss beneath the mistletoe. 'The snow means I won't be able to leave either.'

How she would escape from this house party with what remained of her dignity she didn't know. Half the countryside had probably heard the tale by now thanks to Lord Westbook and Lady Fulton, who'd sprinted away after Lady Frances's announcement as if to inform the entire manor that the house was on fire. Clara walked to the mantel and stared at her reflection in the gilded mirror hanging over it. She still wore her ball gown and jewels, but, for all the diamonds, fine silk, and title, she was nothing more than a woman to be pitied because she had poor judgement when it came to matters of the heart. How Lord Westbook and Lady Fulton must be laughing at her now.

'Lady Tillman will be polite enough not to draw attention to it, but it shall be up to the three of you to resolve the matter as discreetly as possible.'

'All opportunity for discretion ended the moment Lady Frances opened her mouth.' Clara rubbed at the tightness in the back of her neck. It was bad enough she must face Lord Westbook and risk an 'I told you so' from him, but to have to face the rest of the guests after tonight's farce made her sick to her stomach. 'Besides, there's nothing to resolve. She has the prior claim on him and she's welcome to it. He's nothing to me any more and I want nothing more to do with him.'

'Except you're his partner and precedence demands that you sit beside him.'

'Curse precedence, his new fiancée can sit beside him. I'll sit with Lord Wortley.' Clara plunked down hard on the ottoman in front of the fire, the warmth of the flames heating her back, but doing little to drive away the iciness surrounding her heart. She'd loved Hugh once and in their time together he'd rekindled it. For a moment beneath the mistletoe all the possibilities for a bright future that he'd promised her in the last two days had almost come true. Except it wasn't true, but a nasty, awful lie, and this time she couldn't even mourn her loss in private, but must do it in front of everyone here. Curse Hugh and curse her for being so gullible. 'I wish we could go home and leave them to each other. I wish I'd stayed at Winsome.'

The pain of her loneliness was easier to bear than this.

Anne came and knelt before her and took Clara's hands in hers. 'I'm so sorry, Clara, for everything that's happened. This is never how I imagined or wanted it to end.'

'It's not your fault.'

Anne bit one lip and cringed a touch away from Clara. 'I'm afraid it is.'

Clara sat up a straighter. 'What do you mean?'

'I knew he'd be here and I didn't tell you, and then I arranged with Lord Tillman for your name and his to be drawn out of the hat at the pairing.'

Clara stared at Anne, unable to believe what she was saying. She jerked her hands out of her sister-in-law's and jumped to her feet. 'You did what?'

'You know how clever Lord Tillman is with palming cards?'

'Every child here knows that.' He wasn't shy with his tricks.

'Well, I spoke with Lady Tillman about you and Hugh and how much I think the two of you would suit one another. She, being quite the romantic, spoke to Lord Tillman and he palmed your name and Hugh's during the drawing to make sure that you would be together.'

'I can't believe you'd do such a thing.'

'I didn't think it would end like this. None of us did.'

'None of us who? Is everyone in on the collusion?'

'Just Adam and I, and Lord and Lady Tillman.'

'Adam, too?' Clara pressed her palms against her forehead, wanting to scream in frustration. This time everyone, including her own blood relation, had been plotting to throw her and Hugh together and she hadn't been smart enough to sniff out their plans. 'Why do you two always take his side against me?'

'We don't take his side, but because we're not involved, we can see things more clearly than either of you. He cares for you, very deeply, and if Lady Frances hadn't burst in to Holyfield tonight, he would still be there with you.'

'Of course he would be,' Clara sneered, crossing her arms over her chest as she faced Anne, unmoved by her argument in favour of Hugh. Anne might give Hugh the benefit of the doubt, but Clara wouldn't, not any longer. She hadn't been able to see things as they really were before, but she could tonight and it disgusted her. 'Hugh knew I would be here, didn't he? And he knew that I had more money now than even before and I'm free to marry again.'

'What are you suggesting?'

'Exactly what you think I'm suggesting. Everburgh is in trouble again with a potentially long and expensive court battle facing Hugh and a purse incapable of supporting it. I suppose I appeared quite attractive to him, didn't I?'

'You can't believe that he would be so dishonest.'

'After tonight I do. He said Lady Frances

wouldn't marry him because he wasn't wealthy enough for her, but I think it was the other way around. She wasn't rich enough for him and he needs another wealthy wife if he wants to save his estate. I wonder if I shouldn't be thanking Lady Frances for exposing him before it was too late.' Clara shuddered. After all the years of avoiding fortune hunters and less reputable men, to think she'd almost fallen prey to one at a time when she should have been older and wiser disheartened her. In her grief and her desire for happiness, she'd been too blinded by the prospect of finding love to see the truth and it had almost trapped her in a marriage with a man who didn't truly care for her. After having known the joys of love it was awful to think she might have suffered for who knew how many years in a marriage devoid of anything but greed, all because she'd been too ready to believe in Hugh and all his lying words. If she could not sniff out the intention of a man like Hugh, she didn't know how she would guard herself against the many other men who would pursue her for no other reason than her wealth if she ever decided to go to London.

She wandered to the window and watched flurries of snowflakes stick to the panes and collect in the corners. Everything she'd hoped to accomplish this Christmas was slipping away and she wondered if she would ever find joy in this season again. Even the next few days would be a trial, for the trick wouldn't so much be facing the other guests as avoiding Hugh.

A knock on the door made both Anne and Clara turn. Adam entered, as shame-faced as Anne had been when she'd confessed to helping throw Hugh and Clara together. Clara crossed the room, about to confront her brother and berate him for his hand in this mess when Hugh stepped in behind Adam.

'What the devil is he doing here?' Clara demanded, ignoring the sharp intake of breath from both Adam and Anne for her language. They would hear a great many more curses if that man was allowed to remain in her room much longer. They might even find themselves paying for the replacement of a vase or a few candlesticks.

'Hugh would like to speak with you,' Adam explained, more apologetic than demanding.

Clara stared at Hugh with a look to drop a man. He didn't flinch, but met her gaze, as apologetic as Adam, yet unwilling to shirk or shrink under her hard stare. Oh, but the man was infuriating. Even when he was wrong beyond measure he didn't have the decency to behave like it. 'I have nothing to say to him.'

'Then Adam and I will leave you alone.' Anne rushed to Adam, took him by the arm and pulled him from the room.

'No, wait,' Clara called, but it was too late. They were gone and the door shut behind them, leaving Clara to face Hugh alone. She would murder them when they were back at Winsome for continuing to be so troubling. She'd do it here, but she didn't wish their dead bodies to cause any more of a scandal than she was already embroiled in. She fixed on Hugh with an anger to make the fire burn brighter. 'What do you want?'

'To apologise and to explain myself.'

'You needn't explain for I've already heard enough tonight and so has the rest of the house by now, I'm sure.' He moved to protest, but she held up a silencing hand. 'You always have a convenient excuse for all your poor behaviour, don't you, and you expect me to believe it?'

'I never lied to you Clara, and I'm not lying now when I tell you the child isn't mine.'

'Stop. Stop with the lies and deceits and the pretences to caring about me.'

'I do care about you. I love you. I always have, ever since those days at Winsome when you used to sit across from me at dinner, unafraid to laugh at my stupid jokes or join in them with me. All those times you never looked down on me because I had a grand title and not one farthing to make it worth anything. Even back then when I was with you I could believe that there was a better future waiting for me, for us. You were beautiful in your simple dresses with nothing but flowers or ribbons to adorn your hair and you've only become more stunning since. I was a fool to give you up six years ago, but I was bound by duty to choose another. I thought in coming here that I could have a second chance at life, to put behind me for ever the mistakes I'd made in London and become again the respected man who'd first courted you and who'd held the esteem of many good people. And then I saw you again and I wanted more than your esteem or redemption, I wanted you and your heart. You believed in me when few others did and with you I could be myself. You have not lost me. I will find a way out of this predicament and back to you and we will be together. I promise it.'

His unexpected pronouncement almost jolted Clara out of her anger. She lowered her hand to her sides, unable to do anything but stare at him in disbelief. He loved her, but that she should hear it now when all possibility of their happiness together was over infuriated her. She raised an accusing finger, not caring that it trembled with her rage and hurt. 'How dare you speak to me of love. You don't love me, you never have. I've never been anything to you except second best, a spare horse to keep in the running in case the one you're betting on to save Everburgh and your precious legacy falls and stumbles. I won't be taken advantage of like that ever again, do you hear me?'

'I do and you have every right to believe that of me, but I swear to you by everything I have, my title and my lands, that it isn't true. I love you.'

'No, don't say any more.' Clara turned away from him, not wanting to hear these words while everything was crumbling, especially the façade he'd built in front of him these last few days to shield the true man beneath.

'If you will believe in me and stand beside me, I will find a way to prove that the child is not mine and we can be together.'

'No, I won't. I gave you a second chance, Hugh, one I never should have extended and you ruined it. You broke my heart tonight the same way you did six years ago and I'm done with you. Go back to Lady Frances and your child. They need you more than I do.'

Hugh stared at Clara, her cheeks burning not with the humble embarrassment of a compliment, but with the fury of a woman who deserved to be angry. She was right. She had given him a second chance and he'd ruined it, not by what he'd done when they were together, but because of the mistakes he'd made before. It was clear to him that no matter what he did, no matter where he went or who he befriended, he would never shake off the years in London he'd spent frittering away his good name and reputation. With it had gone every hope of he and Clara ever being together. Of all the losses facing him this was the hardest to bear. He could meet every trouble and challenge that life lobbed at him, even the loss of Everburgh if she was by his side to support and help him, but she never would be and he had no one to blame but himself.

Hugh bowed to Clara, unable to tear his eyes away from her as he prepared to leave. 'I wish you all the love and happiness that you deserve. I hope you find it with a man who is truly worthy of you.'

His head held high against the crushing disappointment weighing down his heart, he strode out of the room, closing the door behind him and on every dream he'd ever had about Clara.

Outside the room, Adam and Anne stood together across the hallway, watching him, the pity on their faces as searing as the hate that had decorated Clara's. Without a word, he strode down the hall to his room, carrying with him what was left of his dignity. When he reached the stairs he met Sir Nathaniel coming up from below. Melting flakes of snow dusted the shoulders of his blue coat and the top of his dark shoes were wet from the weather. He stopped at the sight of Hugh, his lips drawing down in a disappointment that had become an all-too-familiar sight tonight.

'Bad show of things at Holyfield, Lady Frances making a scene like that,' Sir Nathaniel mumbled.

'Bad indeed.' The story was working its way through the guests faster than Hugh had anticipated if Sir Nathaniel had already heard it.

'That was no way to handle things, but of course, a gentleman should know better than to find himself in such a situation.' Hugh wanted to protest that the child wasn't his and that he was being trapped, but he wasn't a gentleman to smear a lady's reputation, even if the lady deserved a thorough smearing. 'You will understand if I rescind my recommendation to the solicitors. I can't have my reputation or theirs entangled in such a sordid story.'

Hugh almost doubled over as if he'd been struck in the gut, but he forced himself to stand tall and to show this man no ill will for he was only doing what he thought best, like Adam, and heaven knew how many others. 'I understand and I thank you for your willingness to extend it. I wish I had been worthy of your continued support.'

With a terse nod, Sir Nathaniel made for his room, leaving Hugh alone in the darkness. If he could ride out for Everburgh tonight he would, but with Lady Frances's accusation still hanging in the air, he had to remain. If he left, everyone would think he was abandoning his duty before the matter had been settled and it would tarnish him more than her outrageous proclamation already had. He almost wished he had been a gambler—a monetary debt would be easier to deal with and would confer on him a touch more honour than this debt of the flesh.

With heavy steps, Hugh went to his room, eager to be alone where he could think in peace and concoct some way to get at the truth. There had to be a solution to all of this, there must be, just as there had been one for every trouble that had ever faced Everburgh. He only needed to find it and reveal it to everyone to reclaim his innocence, even if it was Clara he wished to prove it to more than society.

He pushed open the door to his room and stopped cold.

'Elizabeth, what are you doing in here?' He swung the door shut behind him. He wasn't ready to see her again. He needed time to collect his thoughts and her being here caught him on the back foot, a position he did not wish to be in for so important a matter.

'We must speak and now is the best time to do it.'

More than likely she'd crept in here hoping to make a grand exit when they were through and give even more credence to her claims about the child. He wouldn't be surprised if there was a footman or maid she'd paid to have them enter at the right moment and catch them. He would ask her to leave if he didn't think it would create even more of a scene, but she was right, they did need to speak.

'Whose child is it, Elizabeth?' Hugh demanded, turning to the offence, hoping to catch her off guard as she must have hoped to catch him.

'How can you say such a thing?' Elizabeth blanched, having the gall to appear insulted. 'You know it's yours.'

'Do I? You weren't willing to accept me when I asked you before. Suddenly, marriage to me looks very good. It makes me think I'm not so much the father as a convenient gentleman to save you from your mistake.' He curled his lip in disgust at how fast she'd changed her mind about marrying him when she was carrying some other man's bastard, but he couldn't prove it wasn't his. There wasn't a midwife in England who could tell him how far gone she really was or call the lady a liar when, during her travails, she named him as the father. Perhaps one of her maids could give evidence that there had been one or two courses or men since the last time Elizabeth and Hugh had been together. It was a stupid idea. He barely possessed the means to pay for solicitors to defend Everburgh, much less to engage the type of man who could slip a lady's maid a few pounds in exchange for what would be little more than nefarious gossip. He had done a great many things to help himself and the lineage, but he wasn't ready to stoop to such disgustingly low methods to free himself from this present entanglement.

'You're just as guilty as I am for what happened between us, don't think I will take all the blame for it, nor will I be humiliated in society and labelled a harlot for a situation that you helped create.'

Outside, the wind from the storm banged against the window in sharp whistles and whooshes. Hugh rolled his shoulders, the truth in her words as stinging as the cold night.

Her hard eyes softened and she twisted the ribbon on her pelisse between her fingers. 'I realise this is not the most ideal situation for either of us and perhaps I could have handled things a bit differently tonight, but when I saw you with Lady Kingston and I realised that I might be left to face the censure of society alone, and to have my child labelled a bastard, I lost my head.'

'And now you're all but forcing my hand,and you expect me to be glad of it?'

'You and I got along very well together for a time, we could again and it could be a splendid match for both of us.' She slid up to him and touched his arm, the rich perfume he'd once revelled in during the dark hours of night in London sickening today. She was a stunning woman, with her light hair and generous breasts, but in the six months since they'd last been together, whatever allure she held for him had faded. Their care for one another had been a shallow one more of convenience than of any deeper emotion and their time apart had killed it.

'A splendid match for you is what you mean. You'll gain a title much higher than the one you currently hold and your child, whosever it is, will get a legacy and inheritance far above anything that he would enjoy at present.'

She snatched her hand off his arm, her smile twisting to a grimace. 'Yes, I would gain a better title, but one beset by nothing but problems. I know about the lawsuit and how if you're ruled against you'll lose everything. Do you really think I'd pursue you if the child wasn't yours simply to take on more troubles than I already have, to see myself sitting so high all the while knowing I have not a farthing to my name no matter how grand it might be? Do you really think that's something worth scheming for?'

Hugh peered down at her in disgust, his desire to do what was right and honourable tempered by her nasty words. If he made her a marchioness, she wouldn't stand by him through all his challenges, but sneer at and ridicule him for his failures while dismissing his successes as nothing more than something he should have already had. Unlike Clara, she would not help him to see that there was hope even in the darkest of times, nor would she be a pillar of strength for him to rely on when the strain of carrying on seemed like too much. She would be the shrew she was now and some day, if he couldn't give her what she believed was due a marchioness, she would come to hate him as much as Clara did. 'Such loving and comforting words from a woman so desperate to be my wife.'

She drew back, opening her mouth to offer some retort before seeming to think better of speaking and closing it again. She flashed him a simpering smile like the one that had first caught his notice in London. It no longer enticed him like it used to.

'I'm sorry, I don't mean to be so difficult or nasty, but a woman in my situation and condition is apt to not be herself.' She ran her hand over her stomach, but he could not tell through the thickness of her skirt whether there really was a child beneath it. Then she took hold of his arm again, leaning in to him and looking up at him with false tenderness. 'I'm sure that once this little issue with Everburgh is over, you will find a way to regain everything you need to be a proper marquess. You are so clever in that regard.'

Her false flattery didn't move him. 'I'm not certain that the lawsuit will be decided in my favour. Thanks to your outburst last night, I lost the support of a man who could help me. Who knows how many others will follow his lead?'

'Then we will do all we can as man and wife to regain their good opinion both here and in London. I know a number of men who can lend us the money we need to fight the lawsuit and who could help us entertain many influential men who can help us.'

'We aren't even married and already you want me to go into debt?'

'I want you to succeed.' She squeezed his arm to try to drive home the point and Hugh jerked it away from her.

'I need time to consider the matter.'

'There's nothing to consider. You can't leave me in this condition to face everyone's scrutiny alone, nor will I have you abandon me for that woman you were with tonight.'

'She, like many of the other allies I had in the lawsuit, is gone.'

'Good. I'm glad I could show her what kind of man you really are before she found herself in the same unenviable position as me.'

Hugh marvelled at the woman standing in front of him, the one he'd never seen before who was both vindictive and nasty, but in some ways she was right. She was naming him as the father of her child and he was hesitating in his duty to do right by her, leaving her to wonder what the future held for her and the baby. It, and her condition, could allow Hugh to excuse some of what she'd said, but her hard words, more than his doubts about the child, still made him hesitate in asking her to marry him. She'd shown him what a future with her would be like and it made him recoil. This wasn't what he'd imagined for himself when he'd left drinking and London behind and yet it had followed him, like every other mistake he'd made in town.

Hugh raked his fingers through his hair, unable to believe he was faced again with the decision of whether or not to marry a woman he did not love. For all the time he and Elizabeth had spent together, the word had never passed between them because both of them had recognised that it hadn't existed. It had been there with Clara. He hadn't intended to tell her tonight with her shooting daggers at him, but he hadn't been able to hold back. He'd wanted Clara to hear the truth even if she didn't believe it, to comfort her with the peace of knowing that he had genuinely cared for her even if his sins had risen up to consume him. It was a peace he hadn't been able to offer her last time and one she'd rejected tonight and all because of a lying woman.

Now he must do his duty as a gentleman and do what was both right and expected of him. Perhaps, as with Hermione, he and Elizabeth would come to really care for each other. She might mature into a woman who could stand beside him, if not out of concern for him, but out of necessity for herself, for she'd already proven she was willing to work hard in that regard. When his troubles became hers perhaps she would find the strength of will to support him as he needed and to leave this waspish woman before him behind. It was the best he could hope for.

He took Elizabeth's hand and raised it to his chest. She didn't clutch him as Clara had or eye him with the same anticipation and hope. Instead, there was a covetousness in her eyes that made him want to wince and let go, but he held on even while the words were rising up in his throat to choke him. He wanted the love he'd experienced with Clara, the one he'd seen between his parents, the sure thing that would support and carry him through these trying times, not the promise of what might be with another woman, a promise that he doubted would ever be realised. Once again, the desires of his heart no longer mattered. The only thing that mattered was what was best for Everburgh and the Delamare line although he was not certain the child was his. In offering for her, he was taking the chance that another man's child would become the heir to Everburgh and that that man's blood and not Hugh's would benefit from every sacrifice and accomplishment he and his parents had ever made. He was glad his mother was not here to see it, for it did make him as bad as his grandfather.

No, I am nothing like that man.

They'd entered into their relationship freely and parted on amiable terms. If he left her like this, she would suffer far more than he would for their indiscretion. He might not wish to marry her, but he wasn't cruel enough to destroy her completely. He would do his duty and the honourable thing.

'Elizabeth, will you marry me?'

A wide smile of triumph spread across Elizabeth's face and Hugh wished he could take back the words, but he didn't. He might not have Sir Nathaniel or Clara's regard, but he had his honour and he would damn well hang on to both even while he was losing everything else.

Chapter Eleven

Clara left her bedroom and walked down the Stonedown Manor hallway with heavy feet. She'd remained in her room for as long as possible this morning, lingering not so much over her dressing, but the dark circles beneath her eyes from a night spent crying. If she could've avoided coming down altogether she would have, but it wasn't possible. To linger in her room would be to admit defeat and she wasn't about to lower herself any further in the eyes of all the guests more than Hugh's actions had already done. She'd left her jewels behind in her room and decided against wearing one of her new dresses in favour of an older one. There was no point putting on airs now that everything she'd come here to accomplish had been shattered.

At the turn to the stairs, she slowed her steps. Lord Westbook and Lady Fulton walked together a number of paces before her, their backs to her, heads bowed together, their voices low, but not low enough for Clara to miss what they said. They were so involved in their conversation that they didn't notice Clara descending behind them.

'I pity the girl,' Lord Westbook tutted. 'Despite her lineage and wealth this is the second time she's failed to catch a poor marquess.'

'What do you expect from a plain mouse? She might dress herself up in London fashion and Kingston jewels, but she is no better than that country girl who didn't even have the sense to employ a London modiste all those years ago. She might be well off, but she can't compare to a woman of sophistication like Lady Frances and men search for such qualities in a wife.'

At the bottom of the stairs, they made for the back of the house instead of the dining room and their nasty words faded away.

Clara wanted to climb the stairs and return to her room, to lock the door and crawl beneath the covers and stay there until Boxing Day, but instead she forced herself to continue towards the dining room. She had no choice but to put on a good show and make the best of things, to try to reclaim what remained of her dignity. Except she didn't feel dignified, but lonely and hurt and eager for this day and this house party to be over.

With reluctant steps she approached the dining room and paused just outside it to listen to the mix of voices as the other guests chatted with excitement about the ball last night and no doubt about what happened between Clara, Lady Frances and Hugh. Unable to linger here all day and unwilling to have anyone catch her skulking in the hallway, she took a deep breath, composing herself in a manner that would have made her parents proud, and strode inside.

Her suspicion about being the topic of every conversation was confirmed when she appeared and all the voices settled to awkward looks and stares punctuated by an occasional whisper. She didn't chide anyone for speaking about her, but made her way to the sideboard to try to eat breakfast even if she had no appetite for the food. She had to carry on as if everything was not falling apart, just as she'd been forced to do on that Christmas six years ago. Christmas Eve and the annual Christmas Eve ball at Stonedown Manor would be tomorrow night. The next morning would be Christmas and then the morning after that she could safely leave without drawing any more attention to herself than events had already done. She only had to get through the next two days and then she could go home and nurse her broken heart in private and decide what to do next. With the silence behind her growing to fill the entire room, she sensed it would be a very long two days.

'Lady Kingston, it's a pleasure to see you.' Lord Stanhope stepped up beside her, standing much closer than she would have preferred, but having the decency to keep his voice low while the conversation behind them slowly resumed. 'I admire your fortitude in coming down this morning. There are many London ladies who, after having endured what you did last night, would've taken to their beds. I'm glad to see you're made of sterner stuff.'

'Thank you, Lord Stanhope, for your faith in me.' At least there was someone here who appreciated her better qualities far more than

Hugh ever really had. Strange it should be Lord Stanhope.

'You are most welcome, Lady Kingston, for I hate to see someone as nice as you subjected to such an awful thing.' When she finished dropping a small spoonful of eggs on to her plate, he took it from her hands and carried it along with his to the table. 'Please let me know if I may be of some assistance to you for the remainder of our time here. Your new activity partner, perhaps, for I doubt very much that Lord Delamare will have the wherewithal to participate.'

'No, I suppose he will have other matters to attend to.'

Such as arranging for the announcement of his engagement in the London newspapers.

Clara closed her hands into fists at her sides, making her nails bite into her palms before she forced them to relax.

'And if he is so bold to try to come and ruin your good time, I will be sure to call him out and teach him a lesson.'

Lord Stanhope's willingness to serve as her champion brought a small smile to Clara's face. As he set her plate down on the table in front of her before taking his own seat a little of the gloom that had covered her this morning began to lift. Hugh was not the only man in the world and if Clara had the strength to get through this, then in the spring she might have the temerity to endure London, to risk again the chance that she might find love or disappointment. With Lord Stanhope beside her, she felt a little better, but not nearly as hopeful as when Hugh had been with her.

After breakfast, Lord Stanhope's prediction that Hugh would not turn up for the games or insist on remaining Clara's partner was proven correct. Everyone gathered in the sitting room, waiting for the game of charades to begin and Lady Frances and Hugh were nowhere to be seen. In many ways Clara was glad, for it spared her the awkwardness of facing the two of them together since last night in front of all the guests. However, his absence also pointed out once again that she'd been thrown over in favour of a previous lover. It left Clara to sit on the sofa where she'd once enjoyed his attention and bear the many sympathetic looks being tossed her way. Except not all the looks were sympathetic. Lady Fulton stood with Lord

Westbook by the window whispering behind her fan. The craven delight brightening her eyes every time her gaze landed on Clara made Clara want to walk over and knock the silken slats away from her and call her out. However, Clara was not a man to defend her honour in such a way, instead all she could do was keep her back ramrod straight, determined not to crumble or to allow any of the nasty woman's whispering to undermine what remained of her confidence. She must pretend all was well and endure everything alone once again.

To her relief, Lord Stanhope came to stand over her. He wore a fine fawn-coloured coat that contrasted well with his dark waistcoat and added to his debonair air. 'Might I assume by your former partner's absence that I will have the privilege of stepping into his place?'

'I think you may make that assumption, Lord Stanhope, and I appreciate very much your willingness to make such a sacrifice on my part.'

He flipped up the tail of his coat and sat down beside her, stretching out his legs and the highly polished boots covering them up to his knees. 'I assure you it's no sacrifice. Pretending to be a swan or a rose or whatever other object Lord Tillman has selected for us to draw for this game of charades will be much more pleasant with you here to cheer me on.'

'I hope I'm enthusiastic enough to secure your victory.' Clara wondered where she would find the resolve to care enough about this game. It was already taking so much effort to appear before everyone as though her heart was not breaking.

'With you behind me, I'm sure I cannot fail in this endeavour.' Lord Stanhope took her hand and raised it to his lips. He glanced up at her from beneath his eyelashes, the look beguiling and for some reason, at the same time, uncomfortable.

'What have I done to be so worthy of your belief in me?' She withdrew her hand as politely as possible. Although everything he said should turn her head, his touch and his words did not affect her in the same way that Hugh's had. Perhaps it was simply her disappointment in her misplaced faith in Hugh and what it had cost her that kept her from enjoying Lord Stanhope's attention, or maybe it was something else. With her emotions and thoughts in such disarray it was difficult to tell. She was growing weary of all this confusion about men. It made her wish once again that she'd never left Winsome.

'Your mere beauty and charm make you worthy.' He laid his hand on his heart, the gesture drawing her attention to his cravat pin in the shape of a family crest.

'That is a unique cravat pin. Did you have it made in London?' she asked, eager to turn his attention away from his over-exuberant fawning to something more mundane.

'No, it was left to me by my father. One of the men on our estate made it for him. Usually I wouldn't bother with the simple work of country craftsmen, but the man who did this one was quite good.'

'You don't seek to better those who reside on your land?'

'They're hardly worth the effort when it comes to trying to better them. They resist all opportunities to do so, nor can they possibly hope to compete with London craftsmen.'

'But surely your concern for their welfare is one of your top priorities?'

'They must look to their own welfare and

work as their station in life dictates. Whether they succeed or not is up to them,' he dismissed, almost regarding her as if what she'd said was to point out that he had two heads instead of one.

Clara laced her fingers in her lap and shifted away from him a touch, his attitude towards those in his care so much different from Hugh's.

He isn't a man I should be holding up as an example.

In the end, Hugh had proved himself to be far less noble than she'd once believed. Perhaps Lord Stanhope was the better man, although at this moment his dismissive words put him in close competition with Hugh. 'I think it very necessary for a landowner to be concerned with the welfare of those on his estate, for if they don't prosper then neither will he. It's something my father always instilled in me.'

As if seeming to realise his mistake in being so flippant about those employed by his estate, Lord Stanhope tilted his head in contrition. 'Yes, of course you're right, I shouldn't sound so callous about their welfare, but I've had great difficulty with them.

Many are lazy and refuse to do the work necessary to make sure the estate prospers. They don't care if the harvest is good or not and it's caused me no end of difficulties.'

Clara wondered if their lack of concern was because their landowner didn't care about them, but there was no time to pursue the matter. Lord and Lady Tillman entered the room with the hat full of slips of paper with objects to be used for charades. It was time for yet another game to begin.

A new energy surged through the room, but it didn't touch Clara. She was tired of games, especially ones where she had to guess again and again at what something really was. She forced herself to sit through this one, laughing and clapping as required even while her heart wasn't in it. She wished she could be anywhere but in this room, but especially back at Winsome.

At last the game ended and Clara applauded Mrs Alton and her partner Sir Nathaniel along with everybody else.

'Would you care to join me in a walk to the orangery?' Lord Stanhope offered as she rose with the others to take her leave.

'No, I think I'll return to my room to rest

and read. I want to finish the story before the end of our trip here.'

'I hope you enjoy your book and your time in bed,' Lord Stanhope said through a sly smile.

Any other time Clara would've laughed at his attempt at innuendo, but all she could offer him was a wan smile and mumble her excuses, leaving before he or anyone else could think of some reason why she should remain.

Clara went upstairs to her room and sat down near the window with her book, trying to read, but the story held little interest for her. Where she'd craved quiet in the midst of the charades game, it overwhelmed her here and she found herself unable to sit still. Setting the book aside, she wandered from one part of the room to the other, unable to shake the nervous energy building inside her, the one that threatened to bring back all the thoughts about Hugh that had kept her up last night and made her want to burst into tears. Not content to spend another moment alone crying, she went downstairs in search of company. Except when she heard the laughter of the people in the rooms around her, the desire for solitude swept over her again. She wandered down the hall to the library and the illuminated manuscript. She wasn't sure what it was that drew her to this book, but she longed to enjoy the beauty of the words and the serenity of the figures painted on the vellum.

She was not two feet into the room when she regretted coming here. Hugh stood over the book, flipping slowly through the pages. He stopped reading at the sound of someone behind him and turned, the regret in his eyes as powerful as the one in her heart. Whatever it was that had happened last night, it was clear that he was genuinely sorry, but Clara hardened her heart against him. Once again he'd dallied with her when he had not been entirely free to do so and for the second time it was she who would be left without.

'I'm sorry to intrude. I'll leave you to your reading.' Claire began to back out of the room, but he raised his hand to stop her.

'No, please stay.'

'Why?' He wasn't likely to tell her that he'd proven that Lady Frances's child wasn't his and that there was some way for them to be together. It was ridiculous to even think he would. He'd never once fought to be with her, but always followed duty into the arms of another. If she weren't so upset she might even admire him for it, but she couldn't, not today.

'I wish to speak to you.' He stood with his hands behind his back and with all the formality and deference he used to show her parents whenever he would stay at Winsome Manor in between school terms. There was no trace of the swooning lord from last night, no twinkle of humour in his eyes and no hint of his charming smile. Instead, his expression was distant and apologetic, the way the doctor's had been when he'd informed her and Adam that their mother would not recover from her illness and soon follow her father to the grave. It was the same way he'd looked before he'd told her he was going to marry Lady Hermione.

'I think we said all we needed to say to one another last night. There's nothing further to discuss.' Just as before, no questions had been asked or accepted and no promises between them had been made. There was nothing holding them together, no obligations and no reason for her to stay here and endure any more of Hugh and his lies and disappointment. She'd been jilted before she'd even had a chance to accept him and during the Christmas season of all times.

'I want you to be the first to know that I've asked Lady Frances to marry me,' he stated before she could object or leave, his announcement dropping like a piece of stale plum pudding between them. From somewhere down the hall, Lord Westbook's and Lady Fulton's voices carried through the still. Clara couldn't understand what they said. All she could do was focus on Hugh and the disappointment filling her.

The strength she'd employed to face the other guest this morning began to crumble as whatever small hope she'd held that this would turn out all right, as he'd promised, was crushed beneath his announcement. 'Just like last time.'

'This isn't how I wanted things to end between us.'

'And yet it is.' Her words struggled to find their way out of her throat and through the tight air of the room.

'I would give up my title and Everburgh if I could take us back to the moment last night beneath the mistletoe and see it through, to make you my Marchioness instead of her.'

'But you can't.'

'No.' He shook his head. 'Once again duty compels me to wed someone else instead of where my heart is.'

'Stop, Hugh, please, I don't wish to hear it or to know that your love for me is never strong enough for you to fight for us to be together, that your duty to Everburgh or the Delamare line or anything else never includes me.'

'I can't treat her so shabbily, Clara, surely you must see that. I would be less of a man if I did and you know it. If the situation was reversed and it was you instead of Lady Frances carrying a child, you would want to know that I'd do right by you and not cast you aside.'

He moved closer to her, standing over her with the same conviction that she'd faced him with the first day of the house party. Back then she'd intended to dislike him for good and to do nothing more than endure his unfortunate presence. Instead she'd grown to see beyond her prejudices and the London rumours to a man she'd thought was honourable and worth a second chance. It would be easier to forget him if she could continue hating him, but he was right and she hadn't been entirely wrong about him. He was willing to do what was required of him even at the expense of his own desires and happiness. That it also kept being at her expense rankled. She didn't want to listen to his reasons or any other excuses, but wanted him to hurt as much as she did, to experience even a small amount of the pain and humiliation flooding her. 'Yes, I realise you must do the honourable thing. I only wish for once that it was me you were willing to uphold duty and honour to win instead of being cast aside because of it.'

'So do I.' He reached for her hand before remembering himself and pulling back. 'Seeing you that first night here was like experiencing all the hope and optimism we'd shared six years ago. It's a gift I will always treasure and call on to give me strength when things are dark.'

Clara swallowed hard, forcing back the tears stinging her eyes. He'd given her the same gift and then taken it away. 'I'm sure Lady Frances will offer you similar comfort and support.'

The stricken look on his face told her he

didn't agree, but to his credit he did not disparage the woman who was to be his wife, the one who'd stolen him from Clara. For the first time since the debacle at Holyfield she pitied him. In doing his duty and being the honourable gentleman, he was entering into a union that might bring him more misery than joy. It was a fate she would not wish on any man or woman. If she was capable of freeing him from this bond she would, but his life was no longer her concern. He must make his own way now and so must she.

'I wish you all the happiness you deserve and I hope you can find the same contentment with Lady Frances that you offered me during our time here.' Unable to trust her voice or the tears she held back any longer, she turned and left the room, refusing to allow her back to bend or her shoulders to droop with any of the disappointment draping her like the greens did the banister in the entrance hall.

Hugh watched her leave. There was nothing he could do but let her go. In time she would find love again, he didn't doubt it, and he would have to relive once more the agony of reading about her betrothal in the paper and learning about her marriage from friends. What the future held for him he could not say. He would marry a woman he neither loved nor trusted and face a lawsuit in which he might lose everything. The most he could hope for was that the child he would come to love was his and that he could make its future better and its life much easier than his had ever been. This is what would carry him through the dark nights and lonely days facing him, the ones he'd once dreamed that with Clara beside him he could finally end.

Hugh left the library and made for his room, ready to instruct the man assigned to serve as his valet to pack Hugh's things. The snow had abated overnight and the moment the roads were passable, he would leave. It'd been awkward enough this morning inside Stonedown when he'd passed the other guests, enduring their sideways glances of disapproval and whispering. He had no desire to subject himself to any more of it. He'd come here specifically to rebuild his reputation and that goal had failed miserably. There was also no point in staying and causing more discomfort and trouble for either Clara or himself. Word of his engagement to Elizabeth would soon make the rounds, most likely because of her desire to spread the news, and it meant no one could accuse him of shirking his duty to the child. He also had no intention of going downstairs tonight for dinner and putting himself and Clara through the torture of sitting beside each other and pretending that the entire house wasn't whispering or watching them. It hadn't mattered during the last two days when their whispers had been little more than amused speculation about what might happen between them. Since everyone was currently aware of their unfortunate situation, his presence would serve no purpose but to further inflict insult where he'd already caused injury. He also had more difficult matters to consider and attend to. With Sir Nathaniel's help gone, Hugh needed to write letters to other men who had enough of their own skeletons in their closets to not look askance at Hugh's. He hoped they could help him expose the Scotsman for the fraud he was and grant Hugh a reprieve from this last threat facing Everburgh.

Hugh left the library and made his way down the hall towards the main staircase, running over in his mind who in London might help him when a voice interrupted his thoughts.

'A moment of your time, if I may, Lord Delamare?' Lord Westbook stepped out of one of the small sitting rooms, bringing Hugh to a halt.

'What could we possibly have to discuss?' He wanted to throttle the man for spreading the story of him and Lady Frances. If he hadn't been so free with his tongue, the matter might have remained private, but instead he'd made sure that it was fodder to delight the entire countryside.

'Your future and the future of the Delamare line. I couldn't help but overhear that you and Lady Frances are to be married.'

'Do you never tire of listening in doorways to matters that don't concern you?'

'I know you don't think well of me, Lord Delamare, and I don't blame you.' Lord Westbook stepped back into the sitting room and motioned for Hugh to join him. 'But I wish you to know that I sympathise with your situation more than you realise.'

Against his better judgement he followed the man, closing the door behind him so no one else might overhear their conversation. 'You had a solid hand in making the situation worse.'

Lord Westbook fingered his watch chain. 'I do not enjoy a generous income, Lord Delamare, a situation I am sure you can relate to.'

Hugh said nothing.

'I must make myself amiable to people, for if I do not live off the generosity of hosts at many houses during the year then I very often find myself with nowhere to live.'

Hugh unclenched his hands at his sides. For all his dislike of Lord Westbook, he understood the strangling constraints of poverty and the depths one had to sink to in order to survive. For Lord Westbook it was spreading tales that made him a much sought-after guest. For Hugh, it was marrying first for money and waiting for the love to come later.

'I see you do comprehend my predicament. I wish you to know that what I do is never personal, simply a necessary requirement for my welfare.'

'And what does this have to do with me?' Hugh could sympathise with Lord Westbook, but it didn't mean he had to condone his vicious tongue or his hurtful gossip.

'Lady Frances is not the wronged woman she seems.'

This made Hugh a great deal more interested in the man. 'What do you know about Lady Frances?'

'The one thing you need to free you from your present difficulty.'

Hugh stared at him. Was it possible that there was a way out of this? 'Tell me.'

'I will, but first we must come to an understanding.'

Hugh curled up his lip in disgust. 'I won't pay you if that's what you're after.'

'I'm not after money, but a tale. I will provide you with the proof you seek to extricate yourself from your present difficulty if you ensure that I'm privy to everything that happens. A story like this will ensure me a great many invitations and I am in need of them.'

'You want me to sell out a woman to save my own hide?' He should punch the man in his smug face for thinking Hugh so low a man.

'I want to stop Lady Frances from deceiving you and you from breaking Lady Kingston's heart.'

'I don't believe you're this noble.'

'I'm not, but I knew Lady Kingston's parents. They were good people and I was sorry to see them pass. The many times that I've been a guest here have allowed me to watch Lady Kingston overcome a great many sorrows to become a woman worthy of carrying the title Marchioness. Lady Frances is not. I should hate to see her usurp the title from a much more deserving woman.'

Hugh studied Lord Westbook, the sincerity in his small eyes one he'd never seen there before. For whatever else the man was, at present he was honest and his care for Clara real. Hugh must make a decision, but it wasn't a palatable one. Despite having inadvertently done it to Clara more than once, he didn't have it in him to knowingly make a woman the centre of gossip, but if Lord Westbook was right and could confirm Hugh's suspicions about Elizabeth's child, he could reveal her scheming to everyone and regain his reputation and the freedom to marry where his heart dictated. Everyone would see that he was the innocent party and he could do for the first time the one thing Clara wished he'd do—uphold duty and honour to win her instead of having it force him to cast her aside. 'Tell me what you know about Lady Frances and her child and then I'll decide if we have a deal.'

Chapter Twelve

'I thought dinner would never end,' Clara complained, sitting at the foot of Anne's bed. On the table beside Anne, who laid against the headboard, the small clock announced the eleven o'clock hour, the little notes of the chimes singing out in the room.

'I have to say that it was the strangest dinner I have ever endured here. The two most interesting people in the house party were missing and at the very moment when everyone wanted a good look at them.'

'At least they had me there to amuse them.' The last three hours had been as torturous as they'd been the first night when she'd sat beside Hugh. His chair had been empty along with two others at the table tonight. Hugh had sent his excuses to Lady Tillman for why he did not appear with her at the front of the line. Neither Lady Frances nor Lord Stanhope had been there either, both of them pleading headaches to remain above stairs.

'I wonder why Lord Stanhope didn't come down to dinner.' As insincere as she guessed his flattery of her was, she wouldn't have minded a little of it to lift her spirits. Instead, she'd gone without it, slurping her soup in silence like Lady Pariston.

'He probably had something or someone else to keep him in his bedroom,' Anne mused, arching one knowing eyebrow at Clara and making her suspicious.

'What do you mean?'

'Don't you think it's rather odd that Lady Frances and Lord Stanhope arrived on the same day and that they both had some obliging cousin who could recommend them to Lady Tillman?'

'Are you suggesting that Lady Frances really came here to see Lord Stanhope and not Hugh?' Clara didn't put much credence in this speculation, not wanting it to offer her a sliver of hope that Hugh somehow might be freed from his obligation. She didn't care if he was or not, he no longer mattered to her or so she tried to tell herself. After leaving him in the library, she'd done nothing but think about him, lamenting the peace of his presence. He'd been so quick to ease her heartache yesterday and the day before, and now he was the cause of it.

'Perhaps they are conspiring together, especially given that they're both suddenly suffering from same malady preventing them from enjoying the hospitality their cousin went to so much trouble to arrange for them?'

'I doubt that's what it is for I can well imagine why Lady Frances stayed in her room.' There were very few who approved of her way of going about declaring Hugh the father and they hadn't been shy in telling Clara so. It hadn't mitigated Clara's embarrassment, but it had helped to know that people were on her side, except this wasn't a battle because she and Hugh had already surrendered to being apart.

'What if Lady Frances isn't alone in her room? It would be easy enough to find out.' Anne looked up at the ceiling in a gesture Clara knew well. It was the same one she employed whenever she plotted a surprise party for Adam or some secret amusement for James and Lillie.

'You can't possibly be suggesting that we barge in on Lady Frances to see if she and Lord Stanhope are together.' There was no doubting that Anne had gone mad and Clara, too, for even sitting here and listening to this insane idea.

'It would be easy. We simply throw open the door and say we made a mistake in looking for Lady Pariston's room. If she is alone with a wet towel on her head, then we'll know I'm wrong, but if she is alone with more than a towel, think what this could mean.'

That Hugh was right when he said the child wasn't his. No, this was preposterous.

'We'll look like fools if we're wrong.' The whole situation had already left her humiliated enough. Hugh had never been willing to fight for her or risk public embarrassment on her behalf. There was no reason for her to do the same to try to clear his name, except that Anne's suggestion was tempting. No, it wasn't. 'It isn't our affair to meddle in.'

'It involves you as much as anyone else.' Anne rose and slipped on her shoes, indicating she was indeed very serious about this.

'Then it isn't right.'

'Neither is trapping a man into marriage. It's one thing for a widow to dally here and there discreetly and quite another for her to have a child out of wedlock. If Lady Frances is indeed with child, then she is in a very bad situation and will do anything she can to get out of it.'

'Then why doesn't she marry Lord Stanhope if they are involved, as you say.'

'Because he has even less money than Lord Delamare. I heard so from Lord Westbook after dinner when he came in with the men and he's as reliable a source as any. Besides, if I've learned anything from all his stories, it's that most unmarried ladies who find themselves in difficulties by one man who won't marry them won't hesitate to trap another into doing it, especially one whose estate, with a little more effort and time, is likely to recover and become prosperous again. The prospect of being a marchioness, even a poor one, is a great deal more attractive than a scorned woman.'

It all made sense and yet it still sounded so unbelievable, as did Anne's continued faith in Hugh which continued to defy expectation. 'So once again you're taking Hugh's side, believing him despite all evidence to the contrary.'

'Yes, and you should, too.'

'Not after what he's done to me.'

'He did nothing to you, Clara, at least not purposely. His relationship with her was well before you and he truly believed it was over and done until she arrived with her outrageous claim.'

'Why do you and Adam always believe the best of him? Why can you not stand with me for once instead of him?'

'I am standing with you, that's why I'm suggesting this. I saw you at the Holyfield ball with him and at dinner the second night and even during the scavenger hunt and a hundred other times when you were laughing at his jokes and smiling in a way I haven't seen in a very long time. He makes you happy, Clara, and brings back the joy in your eyes. I don't want you to lose that or throw it away because of some London whore making an outrageous claim.'

Clara started. If Anne was using such salty language, then she must really believe what she was telling Clara, but still Clara didn't step off the bed and put on her shoes. She'd already placed so much faith in Hugh and look what it had got her, nothing but grief. If she raised her hopes again and followed Anne in this ridiculous notion, it might bring her more trouble. No, it was better to sit here and let Hugh go, to imagine that out there somewhere was another man worthy of her heart and life, one who wouldn't keep disappointing her and who might be to her everything Hugh had been during the few happy hours they'd enjoyed before reality had stolen him. She only had to go to London and endure a hundred balls, dinners and outings, to weed through fortune hunters and other questionable men to find him. Clara sighed. Perhaps being an unmarried dowager wasn't so bad.

Anne came to the bed and rested her hands on the coverlet, leaning in close to Clara as if they were about to sneak into the Tower and steal the Crown Jewels. 'All we have to do is open Lady Frances's bedroom door and then we'll know, one way or another, if I'm right and Lord Delamare is being trapped or you're right and he's a rotten scoundrel.'

'I don't need to sneak into a room to know he's a scoundrel.' Clara couldn't believe

Anne's tenacity or the way it piqued her curiosity. What did Anne know this time that Clara didn't? 'Besides, what makes you so certain that this is the time to check?'

'Let's call it a woman's intuition.'

Clara's intuition said nothing of the sort, but the sense that another name was being palmed and that there was more to this than Anne simply wanting to get up to mischief made her slide off the bed and put on her shoes. Oh, but she would look like an idiot if Anne was wrong and the increase to her current humiliation almost made her scoff at Anne and make for her own room. But if Anne was right?

She didn't know, but the urge to take the risk of further embarrassment to learn if everything Hugh had told her about loving her and longing to be with her was true was too powerful. It would ease her broken heart to know that he had wanted her and that she hadn't been duped. That it was she and Anne instead of Hugh contriving to find this out saddened her. He should be the one fighting to prove himself to her, not her working to clear his name. It wouldn't change things between them but, if nothing else, perhaps by the time they were done the house would have something else to talk about besides her being jilted. 'All right, I'll go with you.'

Anne and Clara crept down the dimly lit hallway, the sound of snoring coming from behind more than one of the bedroom doors. The rest of the guests were still awake, the light of their candles slipping out from beneath their doors to illuminate the hallway enough for Clara and Anne to find their way. Clara walked along the carpet on the balls of her feet, Anne clinging to her arm as if at any moment they would be discovered and sent like children back to their rooms. Clara's heart raced and a small bead of perspiration dotted her temples when the door to Lady Frances's room came into view. It was near the end of the hall, across from Lady Pariston's. There was no light beneath the old Dowager's door, but one flickered from beneath Lady Frances's.

The closer they came to the door, the slower Clara walked until she finally came to a halt.

'What's wrong?' Anne whispered.

'We shouldn't do this.' It was as bad an idea as coming to Stonedown in the first place.

'Of course we should.' Anne started to pull her towards the door, but Clara dug in her heels.

'What if you're wrong?'

Anne took her by the upper arms, the seriousness in her eyes, even in the low light, unmistakable. 'Trust me, I'm not.'

'What do you know that I don't?'

'Why don't you go and find out?'

The resolve that Clara had almost lost came rushing back to her. Anne had been behind bringing Clara here and then having her paired with Hugh. The suspicion that there was another surprise waiting for Clara that was Anne's doing was too powerful to ignore.

Clara crept up to Lady Frances's door, but instead of taking the knob and throwing it open, she pressed her palms against the cool wood. Inside, the high notes of Lady Frances's voice were audible and it was clear she was speaking to someone. So far Anne was right. Lady Frances wasn't alone, but she could be giving instructions to her maid. Then a man's voice, certainly not Hugh's, made her press her ear to the wood to listen.

'You were perfect last night, darling. You

captured him and gave him no way out. Well done,' Lord Stanhope said, his voice muffled by the wood, but not enough to stop Clara from hearing his words. She bit her thumb-nail to keep from making a squeak of surprise before her wide-eyed gaze met Anne's who had come around to the other side to listen, too.

'Since I've ruined him in Lady Kingston's eyes, she will be much more amenable to your charms.' Lady Frances laughed with wincing triumph. 'You can soothe her broken heart all the way down the aisle and straight into her sizeable annual income.'

'Once I have her money, you and our child, the future Marquess, will want for nothing,' Lord Stanhope promised. 'Thankfully, she's such a simpleton she'll fall for any man who is kind to her.'

Clara gripped the doorknob and, having heard all she needed to hear, threw open the door and stormed in. 'Is that so? I wonder if you have the courage to say such things to my face, you lying cheat.'

They had been lounging in bed, the sheets covering their entwined bodies. At the sight of Clara bearing down on them, Anne following close behind, they jumped apart and, in a frenzy of pulled-up coverlets and the quick donning of garments, tried to cover themselves.

'How dare you barge in here?' Lord Stanhope dropped all pretence to the manners and politeness he'd formerly lavished on Clara as he tugged on his breeches.

Lady Frances sat in the bed, her face buried in her hands in shame.

'How dare you think you can trick me into turning my money over to you or that you could pass off your child as Lord Delamare's.'

'We didn't do anything,' he protested, stuffing the long end of his shirt into his breeches. 'Lady Frances wasn't feeling well and I stepped in here to assist her.'

'With your clothes off?'

'There's no point lying any more for you've both been revealed for the snakes you really are.' Hugh's voice boomed out from behind them. Clara whirled around to see him stride into the room, Lord Westbook and Adam on his heels. 'You thought to trap each of us into a marriage beneficial to you both, one to gain enough money to cover your sizeable debts, money I could not provide Lady Frances, the other to raise up your child sired out of wedlock. Afterwards, you intended to carry on as you are behind our backs and at our expense. Did you really think you could fool us?'

'Yes, they did,' Clara spat, crossing her arms and pinning Lady Frances with a stern look. 'They thought we were simpletons who wouldn't figure out their scheme, but we aren't and now she doesn't even have the courage to look me in the face.'

Lady Frances didn't, turning to one side to avoid Clara's fury as she hugged the sheets up tight to cover her naked body. Lord Stanhope wasn't quite so timid, standing squarely in defiance of Clara until Hugh stormed up on him.

He hustled back, but not fast enough to avoid Hugh who rammed his fist into the man's face. Lady Frances let out a scream as Lord Stanhope went flying backwards, the chair against the wall stopping him hitting the plaster. He slumped to the floor, gripping his jaw. Hugh stood over him, shoulders tight, hands balled at his sides with barely concealed restraint. 'I demand satisfaction for this insult, not to my honour, but to Lady

Kingston's. A woman of her forthrightness and genuine love and care for others does not deserve to be treated so poorly by the likes of you.'

Clara clapped her hands over her mouth. Hugh was demanding that Lord Stanhope face him at dawn and risking being hit by a musket ball and dying to see the humiliation heaped on her by their plot righted. It wasn't his honour he cared about, but hers, and he was willing to place himself in jeopardy to see it restored. He was upholding honour and duty for her, at last.

Rustling near the door drew Clara's attention to the shocked faces of numerous other guests, including Sir Nathaniel, Lady Fulton and Lady Pariston who, having been roused from their rooms by the commotion, watched what was unfolding with as much interest as Lord Westbook.

Lord Stanhope looked back and forth between Hugh and everyone crowded in the doorway.

'What do you say, sir, will you meet me?' Hugh demanded. 'Will you answer for your insult against Lady Kingston?'

Lord Stanhope pushed himself to his feet, cradling his bruised jaw with one hand.

Clara gripped her hands tight together, waiting for him to accept Hugh's challenge, but he did not possess Hugh's conviction.

'If I apologise, will that satisfy you?' Lord Stanhope limply asked, his shoulders slumping in defeat.

'Ask Lady Kingston,' Hugh commanded, the tightness in his body easing at his victory.

Lord Stanhope turned to her, more chastened than Clara had ever seen any child who'd been reprimanded. 'I'm sorry, Lady Kingston, for the insult to your honour. I humbly apologise and ask for your forgiveness.'

'Is it enough, Lady Kingston?' Hugh asked.

Clara paused, making Lord Stanhope shift on his feet in nervous anticipation. She should refuse his apology and force him to meet Hugh with pistols, but she knew the outcome of a duel wasn't certain and that it could be Hugh and not Lord Stanhope who might be killed. To imagine him lost to her for good was more than she could bear and she nodded. 'Yes, your apology is enough.'

'Then we are both satisfied,' Hugh announced. 'We'll leave you alone for you deserve one another.'

Hugh ushered Anne and Clara and the others out into the hallway that was now illuminated with the many candles carried by many guests tempted out of their room by the noise. The latecomers demanded to know what had happened and Lord Westbook was more than willing to tell them a tale that made their eyes widen in surprise.

'What is going on?' Lady Tillman demanded, coming down the hall from her bedroom, her hair in a long plait over her shoulder, Lord Tillman beside her in his dressing gown.

'We are righting a number of wrongs, including every one done to Lady Kingston by Lord Stanhope, Lady Frances and me.' Hugh took Clara's hand and she gasped, the shock of everything including his touch making her tremble. She tried to pull back, but Hugh's grip remained tight, especially when he brought it up to his chest. It gave everyone something else besides Lord Westbook to focus on. 'Before all these people, I want you to know, Clara, that I love you and I don't want anything to ever come between us again. I was a fool to almost allow evil people to try to separate us once more, but I swear to you that it will never happen again.'

A collective gasp of surprise whipped through everyone gathered, but Clara didn't care. Let them whisper and talk, let them call her names and look down on her. It all no longer mattered. Hugh was risking the humiliation of her rejecting him in front of everyone to declare his feelings and he'd been the one to force the apology out of Lord Stanhope. At last, he was fighting for them to be together.

He dropped to his knee in front of Clara, his hands still tight on hers. 'I know I don't deserve you, but I will do everything in my power to be worthy of your love and your life. Clara, I make this vow to be yours always if you will have me.'

He did love her and he wanted her, not for her wealth or anything else, but because of who she was and the joy they found together. In his eyes lingered the uncertainty caused by her silence. He was waiting, afraid she would reject him in front of all these people, but she couldn't. She loved him as much as he loved her. She laid her other hand on the side of his face, the faint stubble there rough against her skin.

'I was wrong about you, so many times, and I didn't believe in you when I should have. I fell for people's lies instead of trusting in what I'd seen for myself. I also placed my need to not be humiliated above the desires of my heart. I love you, too, Hugh and I will have you, assuming there is no one else out there that I don't know of who has some claim to you.'

'I promise you, there is no one.' Hugh breathed in relief.

'Well, perhaps one,' Lady Pariston announced, making everyone, including Hugh and Clara, gasp in surprise before she flashed them a wicked smile. 'But you can have him, Lady Kingston, since I know you prefer marquesses.'

'Indeed, I do.' She tugged Hugh to his feet.

He rose, his hand still tight around hers as he stood over her, admiring her as if she was the answer to every one of his prayers. 'Will you be my Marchioness?'

It was the question she'd longed to hear six years ago, finally being asked and in front of everyone who'd ever doubted how much they truly meant to one another. 'Yes, I will be your Marchioness.'

He clasped her in his arms and took her lips with his, the kiss, the future and everything they'd been denied at last theirs. Nothing could come between them after this and everything he'd promised her yesterday with his touch and the dance would come true. He loved her and she loved him and they would be happy together, meeting every challenge that faced them, confident in themselves and their care for one another. There would be children and many more magical Christmas seasons like this one. It was everything she'd come to Stonedown to find and it was here in Hugh's embrace.

Hugh slowly broke from her kiss, but held her tight, and Clara basked in the strength of his arms around her, her forehead resting against his. 'You must ask Adam for my hand, too, I want everything to be proper and right.'

'I already asked him this evening.'

Clara jerked back, but kept her hands on his shoulders and his arms around her waist, more things than their future becoming clear. 'Did you have something to do with Anne knowing that Lord Stanhope and Lady Frances were together?'

Clara spied Anne and Adam over his shoulder. They regarded her and Hugh with a smug certainness that Clara knew she would never live down.

'Yes. I asked her to help me by taking you to Lady Frances's room. I knew you had to see it for yourself and that everyone must know I was right in order to clear any doubt.'

'But how did you find out?'

'Lord Westbook told me.' He pulled her close again, his body firm against hers. 'I went to a great deal of trouble to arrange this.'

'I'm glad you did. Everyone will be talking about it and us tomorrow.'

'Do you mind?'

'Not at all.' She rose up on her toes and pressed her lips to his, not caring what anyone said or thought. She was with Hugh and that was all that mattered.

Epilogue

Stonedown—Christmas morning, 1807

Hugh watched Clara descend the stairs, the silk of her pale peach gown swirling around her legs as she walked with sure steps towards him. The Christmas morning sunlight from the windows at the top played in the lighter strands of her hair, making a halo around her like so many of the saints in the illuminated manuscript. Behind her, a gaggle of children ran by, racing through the halls and singing Christmas carols at the tops of their little voices to proclaim the arrival of the joyful morning.

Hugh barely heard them as he concentrated on Clara. She paused here and there to offer or accept a Happy Christmas from the footmen coming and going up the stairs, the festive green sprigs in their buttonholes adding to the merriment of the day. It'd been a year since Hugh had first seen her at the top of the stairs in her green dress, an unwilling partner for dinner. There was no hesitancy in her steps or stone-faced greeting this joyous morning, but a quickness to be near him and a smile as bright as the Christmas day. In her arms she carried their infant son, who gurgled and cooed as he sucked on his small fingers, his head just visible from out of the top of the blanket.

'Merry Christmas, Hugh.'

'Merry Christmas, my love.' He swept her lips with his and then rubbed his face against his son's chubby cheek. 'And Merry Christmas to you, little Hugh.'

The boy offered him a wide, toothless smile before making a large yawn, his eyes growing heavy with sleep.

Upstairs, in the hallway outside the bedroom, the other children ran past again, singing Christmas carols at the tops of their lungs and banging on the doors of those still sleeping with cries of 'Happy Christmas' and startling little Hugh. 'Some day soon that will be you, my son.'

'I can't wait for the day.' Clara kissed the sleepy baby on the cheek, then handed him to his nurse. She carried him back upstairs to his bed while Clara took Hugh's arm and the two of them made for the dining room and the sumptuous Christmas morning breakfast waiting there.

'After church, I thought we could take a sleigh ride before the Christmas banquet,' Hugh suggested, the snow outside the front window white and glistening in the morning sun.

'That would be wonderful.'

'Do you like your present?' Hugh asked.

She touched the diamond pendant around her neck and smiled at him. 'I do and it wasn't necessary.'

'It was and some day the diamonds will be larger, just as you deserve.'

'You deserve it more than I do. If you and Sir Nathaniel hadn't fought the lawsuit so well and won, we might have found ourselves homeless.'

'My parents' dream has at last come true. The estate is safe and this year's harvest will make it once again worthy to support the Delamares.' The cold and sparse days of his childhood were long behind him, as was the lonely aimlessness of four years ago. He had a wife and child he loved, an estate to manage and purposefulness that made every day full and welcome.

They strolled into the dining room where Lady Pariston sat eating her eggs, Lord Wortley beside her once more, looking more mature than he had last year. Lady Fulton and Lord Westbook occupied their usual places and huddled together in conversation. Hugh offered Lord Westbook a respectful nod, glad to get one in return while Lady Fulton looked on Clara with a grudging respect that made Clara stand a little taller beside Hugh.

'There you are, Lady Delamare,' Lady Pariston called out at the sight of them. 'The Multiple Marchioness, as I've heard everyone call you.'

'Is that what they say?' Clara laughed as she sat down beside the old Dowager. Far from seeming embarrassed by the sobriquet, she tilted her head to one side to consider it. 'Well, it definitely has a certain ring to it.'

'So does Lady Wortley, but Lord Wortley

still hasn't reached his majority,' Lady Pariston teased, making the young man turn as red as his waistcoat. 'But leave it to you to collect all the Marquesses and leave none for the rest of us, but I must compliment you for choosing the best of the lot.'

'Yes, I have.' She raised her hand to Hugh and he took it, bending over her supple skin to lay a soft kiss on the back of it. He was her Marquess and she his Marchioness and this was their happiest Christmas ever.

* * * * *

THE EARL'S IRRESISTIBLE CHALLENGE
Lara Temple

'And so we circle back to your agenda. Are you always this stubborn or do I bring out the worst in you?'

'Both,' Olivia said.

Lucas laughed, moving forward to raise her chin with the tips of his fingers.

'Do you know, if you want me to comply, you should try to be a little less demanding and a little more conciliating.'

'I don't know why I should bother. You will no doubt do precisely what you want in the end without regard for anyone. The only way so far I have found of getting you to concede anything is either by appealing to your curiosity or to your self-interest. I don't see what good begging would do.'

He slid his thumb gently over her chin, just brushing the line of her lip, and watched as her eyes dilated with what could as much be a sign of alarm as physical interest. He wished he knew which.

'It depends what you are begging for,' he said softly, pulling very slightly on her lower lip. Her breath caught, but she still didn't move. Stubborn *and* imprudent. Or did she possibly really trust him not to take advantage of the fact that they were alone in an empty house in a not-very-genteel part of London?

It really was a pity she was going to waste herself on that dull and dependable young man. What on earth did she think her life would be like with him? All that leashed intensity would burn the poor fool to a crisp if he ever set it loose, which was unlikely. A couple of years of being tied to him and she would be chomping at the bit and probably very ripe for a nice flirtation. He shook his head at his thoughts. Whatever else he was, he had never yet crossed the line with an inexperienced young woman; they were too apt to confuse physical pleasure with emotional connection. It wouldn't be smart to indulge this temptation to see if those lips were as soft and delectable as they looked. Not smart, but very tempting…